A DEADLY CONVERSATION

The phone rang as Sydney started out the door.

Maybe Ethan couldn't get the dinner reservations, she thought, and went to answer it.

But it was not Ethan.

A voice whispered, "Stay out of it . . . it's none of your affair."

She whirled, aware that she'd left the door ajar and not wanting to have her back to it. "Who is this?" she asked, tightening her hold on the receiver.

"Stay out of it."

Sydney thought she detected a mechanical quality to the voice, as though a synthesizer were being used. "You've watched too many B-movies," she said. "I don't scare that easily."

"And I don't give second warnings."

The line went dead.

SMALL
FAVORS

PATRICIA WALLACE

ZEBRA BOOKS
KENSINGTON PUBLISHING CORP.

A
Sydney Bryant
Mystery

ZEBRA BOOKS

are published by

Kensington Publishing Corp.
475 Park Avenue South
New York, NY 10016

Copyright © 1988 by Sydney Bryant

First printing: February 1988

Printed in the United States of America

*For Andy
and
Christina*

Blood cannot be washed out with blood.
— Persian proverb

ONE

It had rained earlier, and the tires hissed as he made the turn from Nautilus into the private driveway, which angled sharply to the right as it started up the hill toward the house. His headlights momentarily revealed eyes glowing at him from beneath the thick growth of bushes.

A cat? Before he got close enough to see the animal had disappeared.

At the top of the hill, a police car had boxed in a Mercedes and a brand new Jaguar in the crescent-shaped area where the driveway dead-ended.

Ethan Ross maneuvered around the patrol car and parked next to the Jag. When he opened the door a buzzer warned him that he'd left his key in the ignition. The sound seemed inordinately loud.

The front door of the house was standing open, and as he approached he could hear voices.

"No, you don't understand," Richard Walker was saying, as though addressing a rather slow child, "my wife wouldn't *do* this."

"Sir, perhaps she went to a neighbor's—"

"What? To borrow a cup of sugar? In this neighborhood, it just isn't done."

Ethan hesitated at the doorway, considered knocking, but decided against it. He found them in the oversized living room. The policeman, who looked out of place in the elegant surroundings, turned as he entered, his right hand moving reflexively to his gun.

"Ethan, thank God," Richard said.

"What's happened?" The message his secretary'd given him had been both urgent and vague: Come to the house immediately!

"It's Hilary. She's gone."

The policeman shifted his weight. His expression did not change, but Ethan sensed his skepticism. From his own years on the police force, Ethan could guess what the man was thinking: yet another errant wife, gone off on a lark, or maybe there'd been a quarrel that morning. . . .

Ethan looked at Richard. "What do you mean, gone?"

"She's disappeared." The muscles along his jaw were tense. "I came home and found the front door unlocked—Hilary would *never* leave it un-locked—and her car's out front, but she's no-where to be found."

"I see."

"It isn't like Hilary," Richard continued.

10

"Where would she go? I—"

"Is her car operational? Maybe she had an errand to run, couldn't get the car started and called a cab, or got a ride from a friend."

Richard shook his head. "I thought of that, but she . . . I found her purse and keys on the table in the foyer, and where would she go without them?"

The policeman cleared his throat. "Mr. Walker—"

"Dr. Walker. I'm a surgeon."

Ethan saw a flicker of disapproval in the officer's eyes and understood that, too: if Hilary was truly missing, now was not the time to be insisting on formalities.

"Sir. Is there any chance Mrs. Walker might have been called away? An emergency in the family?"

"She has no family left."

"Then someone from your—"

"My family would've called *me*. They know my service can reach me within minutes, and besides, I'd be of more use in an emergency."

Ethan tried to imagine the circumstances under which Hilary Walker might have left the house, and a scenario presented itself:

There'd been some kind of an accident—a neighbor's child injured?—and Hilary had gone along to offer moral support to the frantic mother, and, thinking she'd be back before Richard arrived home, had neglected to lock up or leave a note.

"Have *you* checked with your service?" he

asked. "Hilary may have tried to reach you."

"I'll do that now." Richard walked across the living room to a small alcove and picked up the phone.

Ethan looked at the patrolman. Officer Quintero, according to the nameplate above his right shirt pocket. "Have you searched the house?"

"No sir, Dr. Walker said he'd already gone through the house."

"I think maybe you'd better take a look. He may have missed something."

Quintero clearly didn't like being told how to do his job. "You're acquainted with Mrs. Walker?"

"I am."

"Has anything like this ever happened before?"

"Not to my knowledge."

"Would you know if it had?"

Ethan hesitated. He'd known Richard since college, but he was well aware that even close friends kept some parts of their lives private. Richard had never been an open person, and as for Hilary, Ethan realized that he hardly knew her at all.

"Maybe not," he said.

"Most of the time, particularly when the missing person is an adult, it turns out to be—"

"Turns out to be what?" Richard asked sharply, coming up beside them.

"A misunderstanding," the cop said, undaunted.

Richard did not appear to be convinced.

"But, I'll go ahead and file a two-forty-two,

12

and we'll see what we can do."

"And what is that? What *can* you do?"

Ethan put a hand on his friend's arm. "You're on the same side," he said. "Getting angry isn't going to help find Hilary."

Ethan stood in front of the window and looked out. Nautilus Street wound its way up toward Mount Soledad, and the view, looking down at the lights of La Jolla, was spectacular. The clouds hovering above the hillside seemed close enough to touch.

Behind him, Richard was answering the patrolman's questions.

"Your wife has never done anything like this before?"

"No. Never."

"Have you been having any marital problems?"

"Absolutely not."

"Has she any history of emotional problems?"

"I don't know what you mean by that."

"Depression, or has she been nervous, or—"

"No, nothing."

"Nothing she would be seeking professional help for?"

"A psychiatrist, you mean? No."

"She's not under stress that you know of?"

"Everyone is under stress."

"But nothing that she might feel she couldn't cope with?"

"Hilary wouldn't run away from her problems. *If* she had any."

13

"So you're saying she has no problems that you're aware of."

"That's what I'm saying."

Ethan frowned, thinking of how often he'd heard others make similar statements, and how often they'd been proven wrong.

"You said earlier that Mrs. Walker has no family living. There hasn't been a recent death? Sometimes—"

"Her father died before she was born and her mother died when Hilary was a senior in high school. That would make it eighteen years ago."

"No brothers or sisters?"

"No."

"How long have you been married?"

"Six years."

"First marriage?"

"Yes."

"And there've been no problems."

"As I said before, no."

"A happy marriage, with no problems."

"That's what I said."

"Yes, sir."

Neither of them spoke for a minute. Ethan resisted an impulse to look in their direction. Officer Quintero, for all of his apparent reluctance to believe that Hilary was genuinely missing, now was going through the full treatment. The litmus test to ascertain the truthfulness of any subject was how well they could tolerate the silence after a significant question.

People who lie, Ethan had learned, want to fill in the holes around their lies—and there were always holes—with a flood of words. As a kind of protective coloration, he supposed.

Richard remained silent.

"Is there anyone, other than yourself—a friend, maybe—who Mrs. Walker might consult if she—"

"Had a problem?"

"Yes, if she had a problem."

"Mara Drake is her closest friend, but I called her before you arrived and she said she hasn't seen Hilary since earlier this afternoon. They had lunch."

"Mrs. Drake—"

"It's Miss Drake. She's never been married."

"Miss Drake didn't mention whether your wife was upset about anything?"

"I only spoke to her for a few minutes—I wanted to keep the line clear so if Hilary was trying to call she could get through—but Mara said that Hilary seemed fine. That was her word, fine."

"All right. And what time did she last see your wife?"

"I guess it would've been about three o'clock."

"And when did you get home and discover your wife was missing?"

"Half past six."

The phone rang. Ethan turned as Richard bolted off the couch and hurried toward it. The cop glanced at him and Ethan could read in his eyes that he expected it would be Hilary Walker, calling to say that she'd been unavoidably detained and was on her way home.

"Hello?" Then: "Yes, this is Dr. Walker. What? Well, let's try a different medication. . . ."

Ethan looked at his watch. Ten after eight.

The cop stood in the doorway, ready to leave. "You understand, sir, that if we find Mrs. Walker, and she doesn't want to come home, we can't force her to do so."

"Force her? No one's said anything about forcing her to do anything."

"I just want to make sure that you understand. It's not a criminal violation for an adult to—"

"What in the hell are you suggesting?"

"All I'm saying, sir, is that your wife has a right to privacy, and if she left of her own volition, and wishes not to return, we can't make her come home. All we can do is tell you that we've found her. We can't reveal her whereabouts."

"That's the most insane—"

"We can ask her to call you, to let you know she's safe, but that's all."

"I don't believe this." Richard ran a hand through his hair and looked at Ethan.

Ethan nodded. "It's the law."

"And if your wife is still missing in thirty days, you are required to—"

"Thank you, Officer Quintero," Ethan interrupted. "I'll advise Dr. Walker as to the rest of it."

"Are you—"

"I'm an attorney." As he said it, he saw something change in the policeman's eyes. A mistake, he thought, to tell him that.

"Uh-huh. Then I'll be going. Dr. Walker, if your wife should happen to come home on her own, please notify us immediately."

"So what is this 'rest of it' you were talking about?" Richard asked after the patrol car had pulled away.

"It can wait."

"I want to know."

Ethan sighed. "If Hilary hasn't come home or been found in thirty days, according to state law, you, as the reporting party, must supply Sacramento with her dental charts. For purposes of identification."

"Jesus."

"Exactly."

Richard was silent for a moment, then he turned abruptly toward the living room. "I need a drink."

Ethan followed him.

"So what happens now?" Richard poured three fingers of Chivas Regal into a glass. "What'll they do?"

"The police? Well, a report will be filed, and processed through Records, and they'll assign a case number to it. The photograph you gave them will be copied and attached to the file. . . ."

"No, I mean, what will they *do?* How will they look for her?"

"Ah. That." Ethan shook his head. "In all honesty, there's not much they *can* do, given the size of the city. They won't conduct a door-to-door search, I can tell you that. Not for an adult. In fact, I'm a little surprised that they sent an officer out."

"They were reluctant to come at first, but I made a few calls." Richard waved a dismissive hand.

Ethan nodded. "Anyway, the police generally prefer to wait until a person's been missing for twenty-four hours before they take any action. And the circumstances don't warrant—"

"What do you mean, circumstances?"

"There's nothing to indicate that Hilary didn't leave of her own free will."

"Except her car is sitting outside and her purse—"

"There could be an explanation for that. What I mean is, the house is in order."

"Are you saying if I'd messed up the room a little before the police showed up, they'd look harder?"

"No, that's not . . . what I'm saying is, unless there's evidence to the contrary, the police department generally assumes that an adult who disappears does so intentionally. And it's nearly impossible to find someone who doesn't want to be found."

Richard stared at him for a moment and then tossed back his drink. He shuddered. "So what the hell am I going to do? I can't . . . just wait and do *nothing*."

18

"If I were you, I'd think about hiring a private investigator."

"Do you know—"

"I know a good one. Sydney Bryant."

TWO

Sydney Bryant removed the lens cap from the Pentax and braced the camera on top of the car. Through the viewfinder she could see into the ground-floor apartment.

Her subject, a forty-nine-year-old man, married with two grown daughters and a first grandchild on the way, pulled his blond teen-age girlfriend into his lap. For a moment, as they kissed, the girl shielded him from view. His hand caressed the bare skin of her back.

Then the girl moved, resting her head on his shoulder as she began unbuttoning his shirt.

Sydney adjusted the focus and the telephoto lens brought their faces into sharp relief. "Smile," she said, somewhat unnecessarily, and pressed the shutter release. The motor drive advanced the film and she took a quick series of shots.

She lowered the camera before the action heated up. In three days of surveillance, she'd caught and photographed the subject with as many women, none of whom looked a day older than twenty-one.

Her client would get the house. And the car. And alimony, even in this enlightened age. And probably half of the old man's pension, besides.

The wages of sin?

She sighed and glanced at her watch. Ten to nine. The call indicator on her pager had flashed on at eight-thirty, but until Romeo called it a night she was stuck at the scene. Based on his performance the past two nights, though, she doubted he would be—or last—much longer.

"I need a cellular phone," she said to herself. She got back into the car and settled down to wait.

The house on Nautilus was classic California Rich, perched as it was on the side of a hill, sprawling in a controlled geometric fashion, multileveled, with an excess of glass to accommodate the view. Impressive, she thought, but hard as hell to heat.

Sydney pushed the doorbell and then turned to admire the lights of La Jolla. La Jolla, the gem.

The door opened. Richard Walker was perhaps forty, tall and slim, his dark hair showing only a hint of gray at the temples. He was dressed simply enough in a white shirt, open at the neck, and tan slacks.

His eyes were something else again—pale,

nearly translucent blue.

"Dr. Walker? I'm Sydney Bryant," she said.

"Miss Bryant, thank you for coming. I know it's late." He stood aside, indicating with a nod of his head that she precede him into the spacious living room.

"Ethan said it was urgent." She sat on the couch and watched him as he moved to sit across from her. "Your wife is missing?"

"Yes, she ... the police were here, and I gather they'll do *something*, but Ethan suggested that it might be expedient to hire an investigator. Someone thorough, well connected, and ... discreet. I've been assured that you're quite good; Ethan recommended you highly. So ... what now?"

"Why don't you tell me what happened?" Ethan had given her a brief rundown on the phone—from what he'd said it was an interesting case—but she wanted to hear the story from Walker. She turned on her microcassette recorder.

He started to answer, then hesitated, shaking his head. After a moment he said, "I hardly know where to begin."

"You can start by telling me about your wife. About Hilary."

"Hilary," he said. "What do you want to know?"

"Has she left you?"

His eyes narrowed almost imperceptibly. "No. Of course not."

"Why 'of course not'?"

22

"We have a good marriage."

Sydney frowned. "I remember reading an article—a survey actually—about how happy people were with their lives. Married men were the happiest, followed by single women and single men. Married women reported being the least happy. It always seemed odd to me that those unhappy women were married to men who obviously thought they had 'good marriages.'"

"What are you suggesting?"

"Only that no one can ever truly know how someone else feels."

"Maybe not. But I don't believe that Hilary was unhappy."

"All right." She would find out soon enough if that were true. "Is there anything else in Hilary's life that might have given her a reason to leave?"

"I don't think I can answer that."

"Why is that?"

He sighed. "I know how this is going to sound, but Hilary and I had—have—quite separate lives. Separate interests. My profession demands a great deal of my time. The majority of my time."

"Does your wife work?"

"No."

"Did she work before you were married?"

"Yes, she was an assistant administrator at Scripps Memorial. That's where we met."

"Did she like her job?"

"I suppose so, although I don't see what that has to do with anything."

23

"I'm curious how she spends her time."

"Oh, well, she has her charity work." He straightened the crease of his right trouser leg.

"Do you know what specifically—"

"*I* don't, I'm far too busy to keep track of my wife's pet causes." He hesitated again, his expression suddenly guarded, and then said, "I don't want you to get the wrong impression. I love my wife and we have a good marriage, but we're not joined at the hip."

"I understand," she said.

"As for the charity work, if it's important, Mara Drake will be able to answer your questions. Mara is Hilary's closest friend; I'll give you her number."

Sydney reached to turn off the recorder, slipping it into the pocket of her jacket as she stood up. "Would you mind showing me Hilary's bedroom?"

To reach the master bedroom they went up a glass-walled stairway. The rain had stopped, but a fine mist covered the glass, and looking out through it, Sydney was reminded of old black-and-white movies, how they filmed the heroine in soft focus.

To hide any flaws?

At the top of the stairs, Walker switched on the light and waited for her to catch up. When she did, he stood aside and let her pass. He remained in the doorway.

The suite—a bedroom proper and two dressing

rooms with separate bathrooms—was huge. The carpet was jet black and as thick as mink. Oriental-style furniture, including a low-slung bed that seemed as big as the swimming pool she'd glimpsed outside. Japanese watercolors in white frames hung on the pearl-gray walls.

A showroom, she thought.

She glanced at Walker. "Which dressing room is Hilary's?"

"On the right."

He made no move to join her, and she looked at him closely, surprised to see that he appeared to be ill at ease in his own bedroom. "I'll need you to look through her clothes, Dr. Walker; maybe you'll be able to tell if anything is missing."

"I'll try."

In the dressing room the first thing she noticed was a pair of navy open-backed heels that were neatly centered on the mirrored surface of the vanity table. She took a step in that direction, intrigued at finding something out of place.

"Let me put those away," Walker said, reaching for the shoes. "I meant to earlier—"

"Earlier?"

"Yes." He picked the heels up by the straps. "Hilary always kicks her shoes off at the foot of the stairs, and I usually bring them up to her."

Sydney stared at him. "Were these the shoes she was wearing today?"

"They must be. But I can't say for certain; she was in the shower when I left."

She crossed to a pair of french doors and pulled them open. Inside was a walk-in closet, one side of which was comprised of built-in shelves and drawers. The two lowest shelves displayed several dozen pairs of shoes, arranged in order so that all of the light-colored shoes were on the upper shelf and the dark-colored ones on the lower. There was only one open space on the bottom shelf.

Walker had followed her and she turned to him. "Does Hilary keep an extra pair of shoes downstairs? To wear instead of heels?"

"No, she likes to go barefoot in the house." He studied the rows of shoes and then put the pair he held in their proper place.

Strange, she thought. Ethan had told her that Hilary had left her purse and keys behind—had she left the house barefoot as well?

"Dr. Walker, you said your wife was in the shower when you left this morning. Do you know what her plans were for the day?"

"Well, usually she has a class in the mornings—"

"Class?"

"Aerobics. At a private club here in town. Then I believe she had an appointment with her hair stylist; she had some sort of a luncheon tomorrow. Mara will be able to tell you more about that. Anyway, as far as I know, she had lunch with Mara and then came back to the house sometime after three."

"Did you talk to her at all during the day?"

"I'm afraid not."

"So no one saw or spoke to Hilary after three this afternoon?"

"No, or at least, not that I know of."

Sydney looked again at the rows of shoes. "Where does she keep her aerobics shoes?"

"Pardon? Oh. At the club, I imagine."

That would be simple to check out. "Does your wife have an appointment book?"

He nodded. "Two of them. A small one that she carries in her purse, and the other she keeps in the office off the kitchen where she handles the household accounts."

"I'd like to look at both. But first—" she looked around the closet, "—let's finish in here."

They spent twenty minutes searching for anything that would indicate that Hilary might have gone off on her own, for whatever reason, but found nothing. Her matched luggage sat unused on the top shelf, and there were no emptied drawers, no discarded hangers, no cosmetics missing.

In the kitchen office, Walker pulled a leather-bound book out of a drawer and handed it to Sydney. "Hilary is quite conscientious about keeping track of her appointments," he said.

She flipped quickly through the pages. "May I take this with me? I'd like to—"

"Certainly. Whatever you need."

"Thank you."

The notations were concise, and Sydney was relieved to see that Hilary Walker didn't use the shortcuts that people often resorted to: using initials rather than names, or exotic abbreviations that would have stumped a cryptographer. At the back of the book was a section for names and addresses, and these too were neatly printed.

From somewhere in the house, a clock began to chime, and she looked at her watch. Midnight.

"I think that I've got enough to get started," she said.

Walker appeared to be lost in thought, his pale eyes focused on a point somewhere behind her.

Thinking of Hilary?

As they passed back through the kitchen, Sydney saw something on the floor by the sink. Dark spots on the ivory-colored tile.

"Wait," she said.

"What is it?"

She didn't answer. Even from a distance, she thought it looked like blood.

It *was* blood. Three dime-sized drops of dried blood.

In the sink were two stemmed crystal glasses, one of which was broken, lying on its side. The broken glass had blood along the jagged edge. A thin line of blood inched toward the drain but had stopped halfway.

She heard the breath catch in Walker's throat as he took in what he was seeing.

Sydney turned and went to the kitchen door. A smear of blood nearly circled the knob.

Hilary – if indeed it was Hilary's blood – had left the house through this door. But where had she gone?

And why?

THREE

Sydney turned off the flashlight and stood motionless in the dark, listening. The whir of insects, the call of a night bird, and in the distance a siren.

The air was heavy with moisture, and beneath her feet the manicured lawn felt spongy. She pulled her jacket together at the neck and tried to repress a shiver.

Standing perfectly still, her senses heightened by the darkness, she felt a sense of isolation unlike anything she'd ever experienced, as though an impenetrable black curtain had fallen, cutting her off from everything around her.

Had something happened here?

The sensation faded after a minute and she pointed the flashlight at the ground, flicking it on again. The wet blades of grass glistened in the light, but nowhere did she see any signs of blood. Not a surprise, considering the rain; if there had been any blood, it had long since soaked into the ground.

She glanced back up the hill at the house—now dark—and then walked back to where she'd parked her car at the foot of the drive.

San Clemente Canyon Road was deserted. There was no traffic at this hour, not even a drunk weaving his way home. Sydney rolled the window part of the way down; the air smelled of wet pavement.

It had been a long day, but as late as it was, she felt restless. Beginning a new case invariably brought on a feeling of anticipation and impatience. Realistically, there was not much she could do until daybreak, except. . . .

Ethan always said she should feel free to consult him about a case. And Walker was his friend.

After a moment of indecision, she changed lanes and took the Genessee exit.

"My God, Sydney, why aren't you in bed?"

She smiled. "Nobody's asked me." She reached up, patted his cheek, then stepped deftly around him and went inside.

For a moment he stared out at the night. Across the street, a neighbor's dog yipped ferociously.

"Give it a rest," he said, and shut the door.

"Are you talking to me?"

Ethan turned. "No, that damned Pekinese."

She took a can of Pepsi from the small refrigerator behind the bar and popped the tab.

"I wouldn't drink that if I were you; you'll be up all night. Wait a minute, what am I saying? I think I just heard the crack of dawn."

"It's only two, and I'm *very* thirsty." She sat on the arm of the couch and looked at him over the rim of the can as she drank. "I need to talk to you. I knew you'd probably be in court most of the morning, so I thought I'd better catch you before you became, and I quote the ever-efficient Miss Lund, 'unavailable.'"

"Is it about Hilary Walker?" he asked. He sat across from her.

"Hilary, yes. How well do you know her?"

"Not very well, in point of fact. Strictly on a social basis, the wife of a friend. An attractive woman, in a kind of passionless way."

"Do you think she's run off?"

He considered for a moment before answering. "From my rather limited perspective, I'd have to say no, I don't think so."

"Why not?"

"She's not the type."

"I didn't know there was a type," Sydney said.

"You know what I mean. I can't imagine her doing anything so ... dramatic. Or impulsive. Anyway, what reason would she have?"

"Another man?"

"You've been working on too many divorce cases."

"Another woman? Does Walker fool around?"

Ethan frowned and ran a hand through his

32

sandy blond hair. "I'm his lawyer, not his priest."

"His lawyer *and* his friend."

"Either way, he hasn't confided in me."

"I can see you're going to be a lot of help," she said, and then tilted her head back as she finished the soft drink, closing her eyes as she did so.

"What did Richard say?" he asked when she put the can down. "About Hilary."

"That she's happy."

"That's all?"

"Basically. But it's an intriguing case. . . ." She regarded him thoughtfully. "Tell me about Richard Walker."

"What do you want to know?"

"Actually —"

"Don't say it, I know. Everything."

"And whatever else you can think of."

Ethan made a face. "At this ungodly hour, that won't be much."

"You both went to college at Stanford," she prompted. "What was he like then?"

"Not much different than he is now. Even then Richard seemed to know exactly what he wanted from life. Very goal-oriented. Directed in a way that not many of us were. I'd even say . . . driven."

That matched her impression of him. "He's quite good-looking, she said. "What about his personal life?"

"He didn't have one. Too busy maintaining his grade point average."

"That's interesting. All work and no play —"

"—got him accepted to the top-ranked medical schools in the country. Harvard, Johns Hopkins, Yale. And, of course, Stanford. He chose Stanford, naturally."

"Naturally."

"Then . . . well, we lost track of each other for a few years. He went on to medical school and I joined the police force."

"And now he's a client, you said."

Ethan inclined his head in agreement. "He got my number from the alumni association and looked me up when he started his practice here. But everything I've handled for him so far has been strictly routine. I updated his will after he and Hilary married—"

"When was that?"

"Several years ago. I can check the exact date if it's important."

"Never mind. You handled his will and what else?"

"Business matters, generally. I filed his incorporation papers, handled the legal details when he bought the house, and so on."

"He has a lot of money?"

Ethan smiled faintly. "He's doing well."

"How about insurance?"

"What?"

"I assume his life is insured?" At his nod, she added: "And Hilary's?"

"What are you suggesting, Sydney?"

"Nothing."

"This is my friend we're talking about."

All at once, she felt tired. "Ethan, there was

blood in the kitchen."

He blinked, surprised. "What?"

"The way it looked, Hilary—or someone—broke a glass and got cut. There wasn't a lot of blood, a few drops really, but it bothers me."

"Did the police—"

"They sent someone out to pick up the glasses and take samples of the blood, but they didn't seem terribly interested."

"Why wouldn't they be interested?"

"Probably because it looked like a simple kitchen accident. Given the circumstances, a few drops of blood on the floor is hardly cause for excitement."

"Not usually, maybe, but with Hilary missing?" Ethan shook his head. "I don't like it."

"Neither do I."

"So what are you going to do?"

Sydney looked at him evenly. "What I was hired to do: find Hilary Walker."

FOUR

In the red light of the darkroom, Sydney watched the image take shape. The man did not photograph well: the black and white film showed every line and crease on his face, every inch of sagging flesh along his jaw. Dark hair sprouted from the backs of his plump, eager fingers.

In contrast, the girl's skin looked flawless, her body firm and supple with youth.

The second hand on the wall clock completed its sweep and Sydney removed the final print from the developer, rinsed it in the stop-bath, then slid it into the tray containing the fixer. After several minutes she rinsed the print in water and hung it on the line to dry.

She removed her latex gloves and went to turn on the light. The sharp, vinegary smell of the developer filled the small room and she opened the door to let in some fresh air.

Then, working quickly, she cleaned the counters and put away the photographic chemicals and supplies. By the time she finished, the prints were dry and she collected them, taking them with her into the front office.

She put the photographs in a manila envelope along with a copy of her surveillance report from the night before and an itemized statement for her services to date.

The negatives went into the case file.

All that remained was to deliver the material to the client's attorney, who would decide whether additional surveillance might be necessary. She hoped it wouldn't be.

The file on Hilary Walker was centered on her desk. She picked up the folder and opened it. On the right side of the folder were her notes, which she had transcribed when she'd come into the office at six.

On the left side were the two photographs that Richard Walker had given her last night.

Hilary Walker was an attractive woman, dark-eyed, with a mass of warm auburn hair artfully styled in careful disarray. In the first photo, against a studio backdrop, she smiled rather primly at the camera, looking distant, even glacial. But in the second, taken outdoors, she was glancing back over her shoulder, chin tilted defiantly, laughing, her eyes flashing a sultry, sensual challenge.

She studied the second photograph. How

could Ethan have thought this woman passion-less?

After a moment she closed the file and picked up the smaller of the appointment books Walker had given her. Flipping through the gold-edged pages, she found Monday, February 8th.

The entries were written in pencil: an eight-thirty aerobics class; an appointment with Philippe at the Mon Ami Salon at ten; and lunch with Mara Drake at twelve-fifteen. There were no other listings on that day.

And nothing at all listed for Tuesday, although something had been erased. Looking closely, she could just make out the letters C.T. She turned to the previous week and saw C.T. written in on Tuesday and Thursday at two p.m. A quick check revealed similar notations going back to the first of the year.

Oddly, C.T. did not appear in the larger book.

She could find no one with those initials in the address section of either book. Of course, C.T. might not be a person.

Sydney glanced at her watch. Almost eight; was it too early to call Mara Drake?

She reached for the phone.

The storm clouds had scattered, leaving the sky a deep, clear blue. The pavement steamed as the sun evaporated the last of the night's rain.

Mara Drake lived in a sprawling Spanish-style hacienda at the end of a quiet cul-de-sac in La Jolla. A white Rolls Royce was parked in the gravel driveway. Sydney pulled the Mustang in behind it.

A tiled pathway led to a wrought-iron gate, which was standing open. She went through the gate and along a narrow corridor to a small vestibule where a second gate — this one locked — guarded a massive wood door.

There was an intercom set into a panel to the right of the gate and she pressed the "talk" button. "Hello?"

For a moment there was no response, and then a female voice asked, "Who's there?"

"My name is Sydney Bryant . . . I have an appointment with Miss Drake."

There was a sound — a laugh? — and the door swung open. The woman was short and slim, dressed in black silk, with fire-red hair, brown eyes flecked with gold, and a creamy complexion that hinted at Irish genes. A single strand of black pearls adorned her slender neck.

"You are the detective?" The faintest whisper of an accent flavored her words, but the smile was pure Ireland.

"I'm a private investigator," Sydney said. "Are you Mara Drake?"

"I am, but I must've misheard you on the phone this morning; I thought you were the secretary, calling for your boss." She laughed again. "I was picturing someone else entirely — Mr. Sidney Bryant."

"It's happened before." And occasionally, it worked to her advantage to catch someone off-guard. "Thank you for seeing me on such short notice."

"Not at all ... it's the least I can do."

Mara Drake pushed the release on the gate, standing aside as Sydney entered, and then led the way into a crescent-shaped room, the straight wall of which was smoke-colored glass.

Dozens of plants hung from the ceiling, and a dozen more grew in huge terra cotta pots along the curved wall. Several of the plants were in bloom and the air was fragrant with the scent of exotic flowers.

Beyond the smoked-glass window was a formal courtyard, a carved jade fountain at its center. Water cascaded exquisitely over the smooth green stone.

"This is my favorite room." Miss Drake crossed to where two rattan chairs sat at an angle to the window. The skirt of her silk dress moved like quicksilver around her legs as she walked.

"So," she said when they were seated, "there's been no word from Hilary, then?" Her expression was at once hopeful and sad.

"Not yet."

"What a terrible thing." She perched on the edge of the chair, hands clasped but still. "Every time the phone rings, I pray that it's she."

Sydney took the microcassette recorder from her jacket pocket and turned it on. "Her husband told me that you are Hilary's closest friend."

"We're very close, yes."

"How long have you known her?"

"Since she and Richard were married. I was a guest at the wedding, and that's where we met."

"So you knew Dr. Walker first?"

"Ah." She frowned. "No, not really. I'm on the hospital board of directors, all of whom were invited. Richard was the new boy in town back then and I assume he thought it . . . *sine qua non.*"

"Why is that?"

Mara Drake tilted her head, as though considering the question. After a moment, she said, "Medicine can be very political. The doctors used to be kings, not so many years ago, but things are changing. Even a brilliant surgeon—and he *is* brilliant by all accounts—cannot afford to be without allies."

"Or to make enemies?"

"If it can be avoided."

"Does Richard Walker have enemies?"

"None that I know of." Her expression did not change, but for an instant there seemed to be a wariness behind her eyes.

"And Hilary?"

"Absolutely not. Hilary is the most caring person I've ever met."

"I understand you had lunch with her yesterday?"

"Yes, at Elario's."

"What was she wearing when you saw her?"

"A dark gray cable-knit sweater and navy blue linen slacks. She had a navy handbag and matching shoes."

Sydney nodded and made a mental note to

41

take another look through Hilary Walker's closet; she vaguely remembered seeing a gray sweater folded on a shelf.

"How did Hilary seem to you?"

"Fine, as usual."

"You didn't get the feeling that anything was bothering her?"

"Bothering her? I don't believe so. She was a trifle rushed ... apparently one of her Outreach families had a minor emergency the night before and she had to go downtown to sort things out. She didn't go into the details."

Sydney regarded her thoughtfully. "Outreach?"

"Among her many projects, Hilary counsels battered wives. In fact, there was to have been a luncheon in her honor to do, in recognition of all of the good work she's done in the community."

"I see."

"The work is very important to Hilary. She always wanted to do more than just chair a committee or serve on a panel and *talk* about what to do." A tiny furrow appeared on her brow and her voice caught. "That's why I ... I find it difficult to imagine anything that would take her away from us. ..."

"Who could I talk to at Outreach about her work?"

"I'm not sure. They've had several different directors in the last year or so. The funding is very 'iffy,' and the salaried personnel tend to leave when their paychecks aren't honored by the bank."

Sydney had to smile. A few of her clients had

42

paid their bills with rubber checks, but she'd seldom heard the practice referred to in such a delicate way. "Would you happen to have the number for Outreach?"

"I'm sorry, I don't. But the office is near the Senior Center downtown. Tenth and Broadway, I believe."

It was possible, she thought, that Hilary had gotten a call yesterday afternoon – another emergency of some kind? It was certainly worth checking out.

"Miss Drake, do you think that Mrs. Walker went off on her own?"

"No, I don't."

"Not even to get away for a little while? She might have wanted some time to herself."

"Not Hilary. Not without telling someone. If you knew her, you'd understand. She just wouldn't disappear and not let anyone know where she was. She wouldn't want anyone to worry about her."

"How were she and Dr. Walker getting along?"

"Oh. Well. They were . . . things were getting better, I'd say."

"Had there been trouble between them?"

Mara Drake was silent for a minute, absently fingering the pearls at her throat. "No," she said finally, "I wouldn't say *trouble* . . . they've been married a little over six years, and I think, well, the bloom was off the rose, if you understand what I mean."

"Yes, I think I do. Miss Drake, you may have been the last person to see Hilary before she

43

disappeared. Is there anything you can think of—perhaps something she said or did during lunch—that might be of help in finding her? Anything at all?"

"No." She shook her head slowly. "I've been thinking about it ever since Richard called last night, trying to remember, but there's nothing. We had a quiet lunch. As I told Richard, Hilary seemed just fine when I left her."

"What time was that?"

"A little before three."

"Did she say anything to you about her plans for the rest of the afternoon?"

"Actually, yes, now that you mention it. She said she was going to go home, unplug the phone, have a drink, and then do absolutely nothing. I thought it sounded marvelous at the time."

That could account for the glasses in the sink, but why two glasses? "She wasn't expecting any company that you know of?"

"She didn't say."

Thinking of the appointment book, Sydney asked, "Are the initials C.T. familiar to you?"

"C.T.? You mean someone's name?"

"Or a place."

"Nothing comes to mind, but—" she shrugged, "—I really can't say for sure."

The tape had run out on the recorder and Sydney turned it off. When she looked up she found Mara Drake watching her and she had a strong impression that the woman was *waiting* . . . but for what?

44

"Is that all, then?"

Sydney nodded and stood up. "Thank you again for your time."

"I wish I could do more."

At the door, Sydney stopped. "Miss Drake, what do you think happened to Hilary Walker?"

"I don't know. I can hardly force myself to think of it. But ... it can't be good, can it?"

FIVE

The Outreach office was locked up tight. A sheet of paper taped to the inside of the glass door promised regular office hours on Wednesday and listed a phone number for emergencies. No reason was given for the offices being closed.

Sydney used her hand to shade her eyes as she peered through the door. Inside to the left were two semiprivate cubicles, each with a small desk and two chairs. Standard institutional-green file cabinets lined the far wall. A battered Naugahyde couch was the only other furniture in the room.

Multicolored toy blocks had been abandoned on the bare wood floor.

Several lights blinked on the telephones and she could hear faint ringing. Apparently the budget didn't allow for an answering service. No wonder the line had been busy when she'd called.

She copied the emergency number in her notebook. What were the chances, she wondered, that the person who was taking the calls would be able to answer her questions about Hilary Walker?

Even odds?

But when she found a phone booth and called, that number was busy as well. She tried three times at five-minute intervals and failed to get through.

The fourth time she dropped in her dimes, she dialed the Mon Ami Salon. A maniacally cheerful voice answered on the first ring.

"May I speak with Philippe, please?"

"Oh, I'm so sorry, but Philippe isn't in today." The voice managed to sound devastated at having to deliver such wretched news. "He only creates on Mondays, Wednesdays, and Fridays."

"He must belong to a great union."

"*Pardonnez-moi?*"

"Never mind. Do you have a number where I could reach him?"

"Oh, I'm so sorry, but that's not possible. Philippe is so much in demand that he'd never get a single moment of rest if he couldn't depend on us to keep his number absolutely confidential. And if he can't rest, he can't create."

Sydney felt the beginnings of a headache. "That would be a tragedy," she agreed. "But

47

maybe you can answer a question for me."

"I'll try."

"I would like to verify whether or not Hilary Walker kept her appointment with Philippe yesterday morning?"

"Oh, my, let me check that for you."

She could hear the rustle of pages being turned and in the background Julio Iglesias — the Englebert Humperdink of the eighties — warbling a love song. She wondered idly if Julio took Tuesdays and Thursdays off.

"Yes, here it is," the voice said. "Mrs. Walker had a ten o'clock and there's a check-mark by her name."

"Did she make another appointment?"

"Another appointment?"

"Would you look, please? It's very important."

The pages began to rustle again. Sydney wouldn't have thought pages could sound annoyed, but these did.

"I can't find her listed. Not with Philippe, at least, and I doubt if she'd want another stylist."

"Why is that?"

"He's the best. An *artiste*. He spoils his ladies for anyone else."

"I can see how that might happen. Thank you very much for all of your help." She hung up and then dialed the Outreach number.

Still busy.

She started back toward the tiny parking lot

48

where she'd left the Mustang. A wild-eyed old alcoholic — one of the downtown regulars — was sitting in the middle of the sidewalk.

"I see you, damn it," the man said. "Don't do it, don't you do it." He glared at her, rheumy blue eyes swimming in a sea of red, his eyelashes crusted with filth.

A middle-aged couple coming from the other direction walked out into the street rather than passing him by on the pavement.

"Don't do it," the drunk warned, pointing an accusatory finger. "Damn it, I see you."

She walked behind him.

As scary as the old man looked, she knew he wasn't dangerous.

The problem was, she thought, that the ones who were dangerous often didn't look scary at all.

The County Courthouse was only a few blocks away and she headed in that direction.

Downtown San Diego was a network of one-way streets, and more than once she'd ended up someplace she didn't want to go. The direction of the streets alternated, east and west, north and south.

Even the five years she'd spent gridlocked in L.A. hadn't acclimated her to driving the maze.

It was nearing lunchtime, and traffic was slow on Broadway; she managed to catch all of the red lights. At Broadway and Fourth Street, the smell of fast food in the air reminded her she hadn't eaten.

Maybe Ethan would take her to lunch, if she could find him.

After searching for twenty minutes, she found Ethan in an otherwise deserted hallway talking to one of the lawyers from the district attorney's office.

"Sydney, you know Jake Scott, of course."

"Yes." Jake was dark and ruggedly handsome, a civilized version of the Marlboro man in a three-piece suit. He had an incredibly high conviction rate, largely from female juries. The last time she'd talked to him, he'd asked her out. She had refused, politely. Now she smiled, every bit as politely, and extended her hand.

"It's nice to see you, Sydney." He held her hand a second or two longer than necessary. "How's the private eye business?"

"Just fine. How's the lawyer business?"

Jake looked surprised for a moment and then he laughed.

"Excuse us, will you Jake?" Ethan took her arm. "There are a few things I need to go over with Sydney before court reconvenes."

When they were out of hearing range, Ethan said, "Don't antagonize him, Syd."

"Who, me?"

"Yes, you."

"I don't know what you're talking about."

" 'How's the lawyer business?' Sometimes I don't know about you."

"Just making conversation."

"Jake Scott is the heir apparent in the D.A.'s office."

She raised her eyebrows. "Inbreeding is not a healthy practice."

"Nonetheless, he's an important man."

"Maybe I should curtsy or something."

Ethan sighed and shook his head. "You have a real problem with authority figures." He held the door open for her. "One of these days your attitude is going to get you in trouble."

"I have a good lawyer; he'll get me off."

"Don't count on it. Anyway, what brings you downtown? Other than making friends and influencing people?"

"Hilary Walker."

"Really? Have you got any leads?"

"I'm not sure. Maybe." A light breeze had come up and she brushed the hair back from her face. "There's a possibility that someone may have called Hilary yesterday afternoon asking for help."

He stopped short. "What?"

"She counsels battered women for an organization called Outreach. Yesterday morning she apparently got a phone call . . . some kind of an emergency. I haven't been able to talk to anyone at Outreach yet, but what if whoever it was called her again?"

Ethan frowned.

"You were a cop," she said. "You know how dangerous a family fight can be. What if Hilary walked into a situation she couldn't handle?"

SIX

After a quick lunch with Ethan, Sydney drove back to University City.

Her office was located in a U-shaped building that also housed a printing shop, a delicatessen, an insurance office, a video rental center, and a clothing store that specialized in "hard to fit" sizes. The lot was full and she parked the Mustang in the alley behind the building.

The mail had come early for a change and she collected it off the floor, glancing through the envelopes as she crossed to her desk. Nothing looked urgent and she tossed all of it into the "in" basket.

She dialed the Outreach emergency number from memory.

It was still busy.

She considered asking an operator to break in on the line, but decided against it. She didn't want to intrude on someone else's crisis.

Instead she looked up the phone number in

the reverse directory. The address listed was for a Karl Ingram in Pacific Beach. A call to directory assistance verified that it was Ingram's current number.

She dialed the number again. Listening to the busy signal, she tapped her pencil on the note pad, making a random series of dots.

"All you have to do," she said to herself, "is connect the dots."

First, though, she needed more dots.

The private health club Hilary Walker belonged to did not look like any fitness center she'd ever seen.

The Ladies Club building was octagonal, with a modernistic sloping roof and mirrored windows. Inside, the various rooms were separated by blue-tinted Plexiglas walls and carpeted in dark royal blue.

Notably absent was the usual assortment of exercise equipment.

Mozart provided the accompaniment for the club's clientele who were gathered along the barre. Most of the women appeared to be in their thirties or early forties. Even dressed in leotards and tights, they managed to look privileged and pampered. The air smelled of expensive perfume.

No one was sweating.

"May I help you?" A willowy blonde in a black French-cut leotard, matching leg warmers, and white Reeboks walked toward her. A gold name tag pinned to the thin strap of the leotard identified her as Lisa.

"I'd like to speak to the manager."

"I'm the manager." One hand rested on an almost nonexistent hip, while the other delicately stroked her collarbone.

Sydney held out the photostat of her investigator's license. "I have a few questions about one of the club members."

"Really? One of our members?"

"Hilary Walker."

Lisa gave a tiny frown. "I heard about that. I have to admit I was surprised."

"What did you hear?"

Lisa glanced back over her shoulder to where an aerobics class had just begun. "Come into my office and we'll talk," she said.

It was an office in name only; the decor reminded Sydney of a powder room in a trendy restaurant, all blue and gold. Three velvet couches were positioned around a circular table, the top of which was inlaid with mother-of-pearl.

"So," Lisa said as she sank into the cushions, "what do you want to know?"

"What have you heard about Hilary Walker?"

"Well, that she's finally done it."

"Done what?"

"Gone off. I would have left him ages ago, if I were her. But I guess leaving a rich man takes a little more motivation."

"Who told you she'd left her husband?"

Lisa twirled a strand of blond hair around her fingers. "No one told me. But what other reason

55

would she have for taking off?"

"Wait. Let's start at the beginning. Where did you hear that Mrs. Walker was missing?"

"I heard it on the radio when I went out for lunch. It was on the news."

That was a surprise. "What did they say?"

"Oh, you know. 'The wife of a prominent surgeon,' that kind of thing. I wasn't paying that much attention until they mentioned her name."

"Which you recognized—"

"She's in here five days a week for Tanya's aerobics class."

"Was she here yesterday?"

Lisa nodded. "As usual."

"You're sure of that?"

"Yes. She's in the first class, and there aren't that many ladies here that early in the morning. Particularly on Mondays."

"All right. Did she stay for the entire class?"

"I'm pretty sure she did, but you can ask Tanya."

"What time does the class end?"

"Usually around twenty after nine. Sometimes they go a little longer when the mood's right. But that hardly ever happens on a Monday— everybody's still sluggish from the weekend." Lisa sighed and patted her flat stomach. "These are rich women, right? You'd think they'd know better than to stuff their bodies with poisons, but I swear, every Monday it's the same thing. They come in all puffy and bloated. Ugh."

"Do most of the club members change into their workout clothes here?"

"Of course. Into before class and out of afterwards." Lisa laughed suddenly. "I can't really imagine any of them driving around town in a leotard, can you? They come here because they have to, not because they want to. They don't want to be *seen* like that. I'm sure if they could they'd hire someone to do their exercising for them."

"So would I," Sydney said. "Does Mrs. Walker have a locker?"

"All of the members have lockers."

"Can I see it?"

"Not unless you've got the key."

Which she didn't. "Getting back to what you were saying a few minutes ago, what makes you think Hilary Walker left her husband?"

"It seems like a logical conclusion."

"Why is that?"

"Well, I understand he's having an affair."

"Where did you hear that?"

"Oh, just around. Here and there. You know."

Sydney frowned. "Can you be more specific? Do you remember who you heard it from?"

"Listen, these ladies gossip all day long. It's impossible to remember who said what. All I know is a couple of times I heard someone say that Dr. Walker was having an affair and that she—Mrs. Walker—knew about it. So I figured if she took off, she had a good reason."

"Did anyone ever say who the other woman was?"

"Not in so many words. They never mentioned a name, or at least I never heard her name, but

57

she must be Oriental. They always referred to her as his little fortune cookie." Lisa made a point of looking at her watch. "Will this take much longer? I've got a tummy isolation class to teach in a few minutes."

"Just one more question. How did Mrs. Walker seem to you yesterday?"

Lisa stood up and adjusted her leotard. "I don't want you to get the wrong impression. I liked Mrs. Walker in a way, because she was serious about working out. But to me, they're all rich bitches, and I don't give a damn if they come in here crying their eyes out. I can't be bothered."

"Was she crying?"

"Yeah, she was."

SEVEN

When Ingram's number was no longer busy, it went unanswered. Sydney listened to it ringing for a while and then hung up.

"Tomorrow, Mr. Ingram," she said. It irritated her that she'd been unable to get hold of the man. Perhaps she should have taken a chance and driven to his home, but she'd been faked out once today by a misleading busy signal and didn't want to make the same mistake twice.

There was still one more call to make before calling it a day. She got up and retrieved the local phone directory from on top of the file cabinet to look up the nonemergency number for the Northern Area Station of the San Diego Police Department.

"Police Department."

"Lieutenant Travis, please." She sat on a corner of the desk and massaged the back of her neck. Somehow it had gotten to be five o'clock, and the combination of working too many hours on too little sleep was taking its toll.

"Travis," a familiar voice said.

"Mitch, it's Sydney."

"Sydney." There was a long pause. "I haven't heard from you in a long time. How are you?"

"About the same. Listen, I'm working on something—"

"When are you not?"

"I've been hired by Richard Walker to look for his wife."

"*That's* interesting; I was just reading the field report on Walker. It hasn't been twenty-four hours yet, and he's already given up on us finding her?"

"I wouldn't say that."

"Well, as a show of faith it leaves a little to be desired."

"I guess it depends on your point of view."

"Absolutely. So . . . what have you found out, kid?"

She heard the subtle change in the tone of his voice and she closed her eyes for a moment before answering. "Bits and pieces," she said, and then told him briefly what she'd learned.

"I don't know," Mitch said when she finished. "If this woman's husband is cheating on her—"

"Allegedly."

"Whatever. She confronts him and they argue. At first she's only upset, but as the day goes on she gets mad and takes a hike."

Sydney frowned. "I'm not sure I buy that."

"It happens all of the time."

"That doesn't mean it happened *this* time.

Something about it doesn't feel right to me."

"Why did I know you were going to say that?"

"Think about it, Mitch. She left a fifty thousand dollar car in the driveway. The house was unlocked. Her purse and keys were left in plain view. All of her credit cards were in her purse, along with her checkbook and several hundred dollars in cash."

"That doesn't –"

"If she disappeared of her own volition, why should she make it so difficult on herself by leaving behind the cash? I can understand not using the credit cards, because of the paper trail, but why not take the cash?"

"Maybe she went somewhere she knew she wouldn't need any money."

"Where would that be? Shangri-La?" She felt herself getting angry and she took a deep breath. What was bothering her, she knew, was the unspoken alternative – that something terrible had happened to Hilary Walker, and she'd never need money again.

"It could be she wasn't thinking straight," Mitch said. "It could be a lot of things."

"Then what about the blood in the sink?"

"I agree there are some unusual aspects to the case. All I can tell you is we're looking into them."

"And all I'm saying is, I think it's possible that she didn't leave by choice. I told you she had a call from Outreach yesterday morning . . . she could have gotten a second call later in the day."

"You have no proof of that."

Ethan had said the same thing. "I have no proof yet," she admitted, "but I don't think the possibility should be discounted."

"Maybe not. But you know, Sydney, I can't quite see some gutless, low-life bastard who beats his wife as the perp on this, *if* there is a perp. And in my opinion, if it turns out that Hilary Walker didn't take off under her own power, the person most likely to have spirited her away is your client."

"Are you investigating Richard Walker?"

She hadn't expected an answer but he surprised her. "We're watching him."

"That isn't standard procedure?"

"For now let's just say it's not unheard of to take a look at the husband in a case like this . . . and leave it at that."

"I'd rather not leave it at that. You imply that you don't think there's a perp, then you tell me you're watching my client. What's going on?"

Mitch laughed. "Persistent, aren't you? You would've made a good cop."

It was high praise coming from him, and in spite of herself she smiled. "Is that a recruitment pitch?"

"Hell, I've been trying to recruit you for years. Maybe you don't know it, but the fringe benefits are getting better all of the time."

"I wouldn't want to take the cut in pay. But back to my question, lieutenant, what's going on? What is it you're not telling me?"

"You know better than that. This is an ongoing investigation. And I've already said more than I should have."

"Damn it, Mitch." She stood up and carried the phone with her as she paced. "I've worked 'ongoings' before and I've never done anything that might have compromised a police investigation. I wouldn't *do* that."

"I didn't say I thought you would."

"Then what is it?"

"What it isn't, is simple. The word's come down, kid, to keep the lid on this one."

Momentarily at a loss, she said nothing.

"I trust you," he said, "but I'm not the one making the decisions. Listen . . . why don't we get together for a drink some night?"

"I don't know whether that's a good idea. . . ."

"Sydney, Carol and I have separated."

"I hadn't heard." She stopped at the window and stood looking out at the traffic passing in the street. "I'm sorry."

"You don't have to be. It's been coming for a long time."

"Even so . . ."

"It's an occupational hazard. How many cops do you know with good marriages? Anyway, that's just the way things worked out."

"Yes." Outside the sky was darkening and the street lights flickered on. "I'd better go, Mitch. I've got to be someplace at six."

"Sure thing. Take care of yourself. Call me if you want to have that drink."

The phone clicked in her ear.

She was due at her mother's for a bon voyage dinner. In the morning Kathryn Bryant and Laura Ross were flying to Miami for a Caribbean cruise.

Friends from the day they'd moved next door to each other as young brides right after World War II, they had become even closer in the years since their husbands died. Laura Ross was like a second mother to Sydney.

Stepping out into the chill of twilight, she realized she was looking forward to a family evening. She locked up the office and walked to her car.

EIGHT

Sydney followed her mother into the kitchen. "Can I help with anything? Set the table?"

"No, dear, it's all under control." Kathryn Bryant opened the oven broiler to check on the chicken. She turned the pieces and began brushing on her homemade barbecue sauce. "I hope you're hungry," she said.

"Starving." Sydney got a can of Pepsi from the refrigerator and went to lean against the counter. "Did you make potato salad?" Her mother's potato salad was to die for.

"Yes, and cornbread muffins."

"I think this just may clinch your award for mother of the year. Possibly sainthood."

"And for dessert —"

Sydney looked heavenward. "Dessert!"

"Apple dumpling with vanilla sauce."

"I may *be* a dumpling after tonight." She slipped her thumb beneath the waistband of her slacks. "I should've worn something with a little more room."

"You look fine ... in fact, I think you've lost weight." Her mother looked up from the chicken and smiled suddenly. "Are you in love, Sydney?"

"*What?*"

"When you were growing up, I could always tell. Every time you fell in love you'd just about stop eating."

"Every time? You make it sound as though I fell in love twice a week."

"Sometimes it seemed that way." Her mother laughed softly. "Your father used to say to me, 'Kathryn, how on earth can one shy little girl find so may boys worthy of loving?'"

Sydney felt her face grow warm. "They were really only schoolgirl crushes."

"All of them?"

"Well, all but one." She took a sip of her soft drink. "It's funny, but now I can hardly remember what any of them looked like."

"It would be difficult to remember one face out of a crowd," her mother teased. "Your father and I gave up trying to learn their names. . . ."

Sydney made a face. "I'm a lot more selective now."

"That's an understatement. I wonder if there's a place where I can rent a grandchild?"

She nearly choked on her Pepsi. "Mother!"

At that moment the doorbell rang.

"Good, Laura and Ethan are here," her mother said, wiping her hands on her apron. She winked as she passed Sydney on her way to the front room. "Come to think of it, maybe Laura and I could share a grandchild and split the cost."

They all gathered in the kitchen as her mother put the chicken on a platter and arranged the corn muffins in the bread basket. Sydney dug through a drawer to find a serving spoon for the potato salad.

Ethan had brought a bottle of Dom Perignon, which he put reverently into the refrigerator to chill.

"So expensive, Ethan," Laura Ross said. "You'll spoil us."

"Impossible. Two classy ladies deserve a first class send-off." He hugged his mother and kissed the top of her head. "Maybe you'll even think about us while you're sipping that hundred and fifty proof rum."

Kathryn smiled. "A few of those and we'll be lucky if we can remember our names."

"Why not do what you used to do for me whenever I went off to summer camp?" Sydney asked. "Sew your names in your underwear."

Laura and Kathryn exchanged a look. "We already have," they said in unison and began to laugh.

"I may never eat again." Sydney placed her napkin on the dining room table. "That was easily the best dinner I've had in ages."

Laura smiled. "Now, Sydney, don't tell me a pretty young lady like you doesn't go out to dinner half a dozen times a week with some good-looking young man?"

"Actually, no." Even as she said it, she knew what was coming.

"What? You're not seeing anyone? I can't believe that."

"Sydney is too busy," her mother said. "Working all the time."

Laura nodded sagely. "Ethan is the same way."

"Of course, young people these days have different priorities than we did."

"I suppose so, but it's a shame, if you ask me."

"Do you get the feeling," Ethan said, "that we're invisible or something?"

"Or something." Sydney sighed and pushed back her chair. "Come on, invisible man, and help me with the dishes."

She rinsed the plate and put it in the dish rack. "That's it, *finis*," she said.

Ethan held a glass up to the light, inspecting it. "My glasses never get this clean."

"Try using soap."

"Funny." He swatted at her with the towel. "Our mothers would say you need a wife."

"I had a wife," he said dryly. "My glasses still weren't clean."

"Speaking of which, what do you make of the fact that there were two of them?"

"What are you talking about? Who had two wives?"

She shook her head. "Two glasses, counselor.

In the sink at Walker's house."

"Oh. That. I hadn't really given it much thought."

"I sure would be interested to know who was there that afternoon." She sat at the kitchen table, watching him as he worked. "Hilary was out all morning and didn't get back to the house until after three. By six-thirty she had vanished. Maybe whoever was at the house knows what happened to her."

"Why wouldn't they come forward? It's been on the news. . . ."

"I don't know. Unless, of course, whoever it was had something to do with her disappearance."

"That would mean it was someone she knew and liked well enough to offer them a drink." He frowned. "Someone she trusted."

Sydney regarded him thoughtfully. "I wonder if the police lifted any prints off those glasses?"

"Even if they did, it's a little early for a match, even with their new computer identification system." Ethan folded the dish towel and put it away. "But you have connections at the police department, why don't you ask them?"

"I'm not sure they'd tell me."

"Why not?"

"They're not talking."

He sat across from her. "They know you're working for Richard?"

"Yes."

"Well then, you're on your own. It's a legend among policemen: if something happens to the

69

wife of a doctor, he's the prime suspect."

"Why is that?"

"Doctors make good killers."

"I'll keep that in mind."

"On the other hand, if they really suspected him, they would have conducted a more thorough search of the house."

"I wonder. But, now that you mention it, I'd like to go through the house again myself."

"I'm sure that can be arranged—"

The swinging door pushed open. "All right, you two," her mother said. "We figured we'd find you in here talking about work. That's enough of that ... it's time for the champagne."

Ethan raised his eyebrows. "I'll give Richard a call in the morning," he whispered as they got up from the table.

"I heard that, Ethan Daniel Ross." Laura shook a finger at them. "Honestly, we can't leave you alone for a minute. Kathryn, I don't think the younger generation knows a thing about having a good time."

Heat from the fireplace made her sleepy.

Sydney watched the champagne bubbles rising in the glass and imagined them doing the same in her head. It took an effort to keep her eyes open.

"I've always wanted to visit St. Thomas," her mother said. "How different it must be to live on an island, away from all of this."

"A simple life." Laura Ross sounded wistful.

70

"Without distractions."

"Being lulled to sleep by the waves breaking on the beach. ..."

"Caressed by a gentle tropical breeze. ..."

"The night sky brilliant with stars. ..."

Ethan laughed. "Mosquitos the size of small dogs. ..."

Sydney smiled and finished her champagne. She twirled the stem of the glass slowly between her thumb and forefinger and watched the light from the fire reflecting off the faceted surface.

I'll just close my eyes for a minute, she thought.

The sound of voices began to fade and she curled further into the soft cushions of the love-seat.

"Sydney."

"Hmm?"

"Come on, I'll help you upstairs."

She felt herself being lifted and she opened her eyes. The fire had died down and the living room was dimly lit.

"What? Ethan, what ..."

"You fell asleep."

"Oh. The champagne. I should never drink champagne."

"You had one glass."

"That's all it takes." She rested her head on his shoulder. "The room is spinning."

"Poor baby. Come on, let's get you to bed."

"I can walk," she said.

71

"Sure you can." He tightened his hold on her and in a second he was carrying her up the stairs.

All of it so familiar. The third stair from the top creaked as it always had. A patchwork of moonlight shining through the trellis outside her bedroom window. The lingering scent of the floral sachets her mother used in the closets.

He lowered her onto the bed and tucked the comforter around her. "Go back to sleep."

"Ethan?"

He stopped at the door and turned to look at her. "What is it?"

"Thank you for taking me to bed."

"Any time," he said and was gone.

NINE

The smell of fresh-ground coffee woke her. She never had acquired a taste for the stuff, but the aroma was nearly irresistible.

The pale light streaming through the windows indicated it was early morning. For a moment she felt disoriented, and she sat up, pushing the hair back out of her eyes.

She was in her old bedroom. In spite of the time that had passed since she'd lived here, she had a strong sense of belonging.

Twenty-one years' worth of memories.

After her father died, her mother had talked of selling the place and buying something smaller where she wouldn't "rattle around." Sydney had kept silent, knowing how unfair it would be to urge her mother to stay in a house she herself had left, but she'd been greatly relieved when the decision was made not to sell.

She turned back the comforter and got out of bed. During the night she'd taken off her slacks and blouse, and she found them on the window seat where she'd always tossed her clothes. A little wrinkled, but they'd do until she could get to the apartment and change.

"Oh, I hope I didn't wake you," her mother said when she came into the kitchen. "You looked so tired last night ... I thought you might want to sleep in this morning."

Sydney shook her head. "I'm fine."

"Do you want breakfast?"

"No, thanks." She sat at the kitchen table and pulled the newspaper toward her.

"The taxi will be here any minute, but I can scramble an egg. ..."

"Really, Mom, I couldn't eat a thing. But why on earth did you call a cab? I can drive you and Mrs. Ross to the airport."

"You know how I hate good-byes at airports."

Sydney smiled. "I remember."

"Anyway, you need your sleep."

"I'm awake now," she said absently. The studio photograph of Hilary Walker was on the second page of the *San Diego Union* and she scanned the brief article. A quote from an unidentified source indicated that the police were "actively looking into every possibility that might explain Mrs. Walker's disappearance."

"You know, Sydney," her mother said, placing a glass of orange juice in front of her, "I think you work way too hard at this job."

"It's not a job." She glanced up from the

74

paper. "It's my business."

"Semantics. What difference does it make what you call it? You're working much too hard." Kathryn Bryant sat down at the table and put her hand over her daughter's. "Honey, you were exhausted last night. Do you know what time you fell asleep? Eight-thirty. Eight-*thirty*! You haven't willingly gone to sleep that early since you were seven years old."

"I know, but—"

"—you're on a new case. Yes, Ethan told me about that. But when you've finished this one, there'll be another."

Sydney smiled. "God, I hope so."

"And you'll work just as obsessively on the next case, and then there'll be another and another."

"I don't think I'm being obsessive. Besides, I took a night off, didn't I?"

"Did you?"

"Mother, I was here . . . I didn't make a single call."

"But you *did* talk to Ethan about the investigation. And I can always tell when your mind is elsewhere."

"I can't help that. That's just the way I am."

"All I'm saying, honey, is you need to take some time off."

Sydney traced a question mark in the condensation that had formed on the orange juice glass. "After this one," she said.

Her mother sighed and squeezed her hand. "I remember when you were a little girl, and every year at Easter, long after all of the other children had given up, you'd still be hunting for that last Easter egg."

"But I found it, didn't I?"

"Yes, honey, you found it."

Sydney stood waving as the cab drove away. When it had disappeared from view she walked slowly to her car.

It had gotten cold during the night and the windshield was beaded with dew. She started the engine and turned on the wipers, then waited for the car to warm up.

She'd left her pager on the console, and she saw that the call indicator light was lit.

"Damn." Had she missed an important call?

She had her a set of keys to the house and she dug them out of her shoulder bag. She killed the engine, pulled the key out of the ignition, and ran back to the porch.

Inside she went directly to the phone and dialed her service.

An unfamiliar voice answered.

"This is Sydney Bryant, Bryant Investigations. You have a call for me?"

"One moment, I'll check."

The line went silent and then she heard a series of clicks.

"Sydney? It's Daphne." Daphne was the night operator, the most efficient of the lot of them. "Listen, this call came in about five this morning. I tried your home and the office, but—"

"I know. I forgot to leave this number. What is it?"

"A Dr. Richard Walker called and said it was urgent that he speak with you. Do you want me to try and connect you?"

Sydney glanced at her watch; it was after seven and Daphne was officially off duty. "No, that's all right. What number did he leave?"

"A couple, actually. Do you have a pencil handy?"

She copied down the numbers, reading them back for verification. "Thanks, Daphne."

"No problem. I know you're in a rush, so I'll just say, good for you."

"Good for me?"

"You didn't spend the night in your own bed, and you definitely weren't working."

"Tell that to my mother," Sydney said, but the line had already gone dead.

Walker didn't answer at home, so she dialed the second number.

"Scripps Memorial."

"Dr. Richard Walker, please."

"One moment, I'll page him for you."

After a brief interval the line began to ring again. This time a British-accented voice answered. "Surgery."

"I'm trying to locate Dr. Richard Walker."

"The doctor is in the scrub room. May I take a message?"

"It's rather important; I'm returning his call."

"And you are . . .?"

"Sydney Bryant."

"Hold on, then. I'll see if I can catch him before he pops into the O.R."

She smiled at the image of the urbane Dr. Walker "popping" anywhere.

When he came on the line, Walker sounded as if he were talking from inside an echo chamber. She could hear running water in the background.

"Miss Bryant," he said. "What in the hell is going on?"

Before she could ask what he was referring to he continued:

"There was a reporter camped out on my doorstep when I got home last night."

"What time was this?"

"God, I don't know. I'd been in surgery half the night, I suppose it was after three. Regardless, the man had the nerve to insinuate that I had not been completely forthcoming when I reported Hilary missing on Monday night."

Her own dealings with the press had generally been satisfactory, but she knew of a few reporters who reacted like pit bulls to the scent of blood.

"What exactly did he say?"

"It wasn't so much *what* he said but the nasty way he said it. That and the expression on his face. As though he knows more about what's going on than I do. I want to know where the hell he's getting his information."

Sydney frowned, thinking of what Mitch Tra-

78

vis had told her. Occasionally, for reasons known only to the privileged few, the police department would leak information to the press. "Did you get the reporter's name?"

"I don't recall the bastard's name, but he gave me his card." In the background a voice spoke, the urgency plain although the words were not. "I'll be right there," Walker said, and then to her: "I'm due in surgery, so I haven't time to discuss this any further. But I want you to look into it."

"I will, but I'll need a name."

"Come down to the hospital, then. I'll have someone find the card and you can pick it up at the desk."

TEN

Sydney arrived at the hospital forty-five minutes later after a brief stop at her apartment for a shower and change of clothes.

The nurse at the surgery information desk was not the one she'd spoken to on the phone. "I'm sorry, but if you're looking for Dr. Walker it may be a while. He's already in the operating room."

"He was supposed to leave something at the desk for me."

"Well, then, it must be here." The woman reached for a small stack of envelopes. "The trick is finding it. What did you say your name is?"

"Sydney Bryant."

"That's an unusual name," the nurse said as she rifled through the envelopes. "My grandmother had a theory that people grow to resemble their names. Every Calvin I've ever met *looked* like a Calvin, if you know what I mean.

But Sydney ... I wouldn't have guessed it."

"Thank you ... I think."

"Wait a minute, here it is." The woman handed her a sealed envelope.

"May I leave a message for him?" Ethan had promised he would call Walker to arrange for her to conduct another search of the house, but she preferred not to leave anything to chance.

"Sure, although I have to warn you it may be several hours before he'll get it; he's scheduled to be in O.R. for the remainder of the morning."

"I understand." She wrote a short note asking him to call her and included her answering service's number so that he could have her paged.

Sydney tore open the envelope as she walked along the hallway and extracted the business card. She flipped it over to read the printed side and stopped short.

The reporter was Victor Griffith, a local stringer for one of the national wire services.

"Surprise, surprise," she said, but in truth she wasn't at all surprised. Irritated, but not surprised.

Still only in his early twenties, Victor Griffith had become something of a legend among newspeople for always being in the right place at the right time.

The man acted as a kind of divining rod for detecting tragedy. With frightening regularity, he beat the police to the scenes of major accidents. He showed up at fires long before the first siren signaled the arrival of the fire trucks. The Coronado Bridge had become a magnet for potential jumpers, and Griffith's pawnshop camera had captured more than one in midleap. Narcotics officers making arrests of drug dealers — where secrecy was of utmost importance — were grudgingly resigned to having him underfoot. A few of the hard-core law-and-order types had threatened to arrest him on sight.

His instinct for breaking news was phenomenal. Plane crashes, lost children, border incidents, drive-by shootings, white collar crime, or political wrongdoing; all of it was grist for his word mill.

His instinct for fair play was nonexistent.

Griffith showing up was a complication she didn't need. His interest in Richard Walker was not a good sign.

Where there's smoke, she thought.

She found Victor Griffith in a corner booth at a small donut shop on Balboa Avenue where he usually held court when he wasn't twitching after a story.

If the nurse's grandmother was right, Griffith should have been named Ichabod; he was nearly six and a half feet tall and painfully thin. His arms extended several inches beyond the cuffs of his off-the-rack sports coat, and his neck seemed abnormally long. He had thinning brown hair, which he wore in a Prince Valiant cut, and pale-lashed hazel eyes.

He was admiring a jelly donut when she sat down across from him.

"Raspberry," he said, and took a huge bite, eating vigorously and with obvious appreciation. A glob of jelly escaped to the corner of his mouth and he licked it off, then grinned at her. "Hungry?"

"I'll pass."

"You don't know what you're missing." He stuffed the rest of donut into his mouth and talked around it. "So, how's my favorite private dick?"

"Just great."

"Getting a lot of work, or so I hear." He wet the tip of his index finger with his tongue and dabbed at the bits of sugar glaze that had fallen on the smeared surface of the table.

Sydney worked at keeping from showing her distaste; Griffith loved to play games, and "gross-out" was one of his favorites. "I keep busy," she said.

"God, yes. Working for Richard Walker? That'd keep me up at nights."

"That's what my client tells me."

His eyes showed mock surprise. "He actually told you I went to see him?"

"Come off it, Griffith. You gave him your card knowing full well he'd pass it on to me."

"Maybe."

She smiled and shook her head. "Maybe, my ass. You knew I wouldn't talk to you if you showed up and started asking questions, so you arranged for Walker to get *me* to come to *you.*"

"Am I that clever?"

"You must be; here I am."

"And here we are." He leaned back and laced his fingers behind his head. "So ... go ahead and grill me. Give me a little heat."

Another of his games.

Sydney glanced at her watch; she wanted to be downtown when the Outreach office opened. "I really don't have time for this. You wouldn't answer any of my questions any more than I'd answer yours. Why don't you just tell me what it is you want?"

"What does every journalist want? The truth, the whole truth, and nuttin' but the truth."

"That certainly is a noble aspiration, all right. But do you think you can uncover the truth on Walker's doorstep at three o'clock in the morning?"

"Sweet thing, I figure I can get the truth by keeping an eye on you. You know, I am by nature a lazy man. I detest having to work late at night, but it was necessary to get the good doctor's attention."

"You did that."

His smile was modest. "I have my moments ... but I digress. I don't mind telling you I was pleased to hear that you were working on this lady's disappearance—"

"Who told you I was?"

"Now, now ... I can't reveal my sources." He winked at her. "Even if you stripped me naked and tortured me."

"In your dreams."

Griffith laughed. "Night after night after night! But, as I was saying, with you working the Walker case I figure I can sit back and take it easy."

"Really." She studied him for a moment. "Something's wrong here. I get the terrible feeling you think I'm going to feed you the story out of this."

He inclined his head in agreement. "There you go."

"Why would I want to do that? We've always been at cross purposes—"

"I can overlook that."

"What makes you think I can?"

"Because I have information that you might find of interest."

"Such as?"

"Sydney! I can't just *tell* you. There are certain formalities that have to be observed. We are, after all, professionals. First we come to an agreement, and *then* I'll let you pick my brain."

"I don't think so." She stood up. "I don't know who your source is or what information you have, but I don't trust you."

His hand clutched at his chest. "I'm hurt. No, I'm mortally wounded. You don't trust me?"

"On a slow news day you'd hand a gun to a crazy man and hope like hell he'd shoot somebody. We both know you'd do anything for a story."

"Hey, that's my job." He looked offended.

"And you're good at it. The best I've ever seen. But I'm not going to load the gun for you or

85

anyone else. What I find out about Hilary Walker is not for public release—"

"Unless," he said, "unless—"

She finished for him: "Unless a crime has been committed, in which instance I'll give whatever information I uncover to the police, not to the press."

"I think you're being ... being ..."

"The word is ethical."

"Spare me. If you don't want to work together, I guess that's that." Griffith shrugged. "But, you know, I'll be watching."

"There's nothing I can do about that, but don't expect me to make it easy for you." Sydney started to leave and then hesitated, turning to face him once more. "Walker's an influential man," she said. "If I were you, I'd be careful not to cross him."

"He's the one who'd better be careful."

ELEVEN

Traffic was light, and Sydney made it downtown just after ten a.m. The small lot where she'd parked the day before was full; she circled it twice before pulling back into the street and finding a metered space.

A bell jangled as she pushed open the door to the Outreach office. The women who were waiting turned to look at her as she stepped inside. A dark-eyed little girl of about three turned her face into her mother's skirt.

No one spoke.

Only one of the desks was occupied, and the man who sat at it did not raise his eyes to see who had come in. He used the eraser of his pencil to page through an untidy sheath of papers, all the while shaking his head.

"Where's the copy of your original AFDC application? I don't see it here."

The young woman who sat in the client chair stared at him blankly. "Is all there."

"It isn't here."

"All the papers," she insisted.

"I can't get you into the shelter without verification of eligibility."

"I brought."

"I'm sorry," he said, and held the papers out to her. "You'll have to go to the welfare office and get the rest of your paperwork. If you hurry, I still might be able to do something for you today."

"Is no hurry at welfare." With a sigh, the young woman got up from the chair.

The others began to whisper among themselves.

Sydney moved so the young woman could pass by. The bell jangled and the door closed.

"Who's next?" The man glanced around the room, but when he saw her he frowned.

He looked, she thought, like John Lithgow. "Are you Karl Ingram?" she asked.

"Yes."

She was aware that the whispering had stopped and all eyes were watching them. "My name is Sydney Bryant and I'm a private investigator. I have a few questions I'd like to ask when you have a moment."

He raised his eyebrows. "You can see I've got my hands full right now."

"I don't mind waiting."

Ingram worked methodically—scanning paperwork, making calls, writing vouchers—and by eleven-thirty, he'd finished with the last client.

"I'm sorry this took so long," he said, getting up to lock the door. "The problem is, it never really stops. There'll be another group waiting when I come back from lunch."

"I had no idea..."

"It isn't something that gets a lot of attention." He gestured for her to sit across from him. "They are, by and large, quiet victims. So quiet that sometimes they die before we become aware of them."

"Yes." None of the women had spoken directly of what caused them to seek help, but she had heard the resignation in their voices and had seen the bruises, which they made no attempt to hide.

It made her incredibly sad.

"Now ... you had some questions."

She turned on her recorder. "Mr. Ingram, have you heard about Hilary Walker's disappearance?"

"Why, yes. It was on the late news last night." The corners of his mouth turned down and he lowered his voice to a whisper. "I was shocked, I must tell you."

"I've been hired to try to find her."

"Aren't the police ... looking for her?"

Sydney nodded. "But in a case like this, it's not unusual for the family to hire a private investigator to conduct a parallel investigation."

"A case like this," he echoed. "I have few illusions anymore, but I can hardly believe such a thing could happen. At least, not to Hilary—Mrs. Walker, that is. She is a wonderful woman; I think the world of her. Everyone here does. And she is absolutely the best volunteer I've ever encountered. Not a dilettante; she's *involved*, in the purest sense of the word."

"How long have you known her?"

"Ever since I was hired as director. That'd be eight months now."

"And you feel you know her well?"

"Yes. We spent quite a lot of time together. Her schedule was flexible, but she frequently worked after hours—as I do—and she was one of the few who didn't mind working weekends."

"What can you tell me about her work?"

"You mean, what were her duties? Well, generally the counselors work in the field, doing all of the follow-up on our cases once the woman has left the shelter. They make home visits, act as an advocate with the police and the court if any legal action is being taken, and otherwise provide moral support."

"Is there any danger involved in the field work?"

"To be honest, yes." A tic played at the corner of Ingram's right eye. "These men are bullies. They think it's their God-given right to keep the little woman in line, even if it requires breaking some bones. They don't take kindly to anyone's interfering in their sordid, futile lives." He spoke without apparent emotion, but the words had the impact of a physical blow.

Sydney felt a sense of dread. "I've been told

that Mrs. Walker received a call Monday morning from one of her Outreach clients."

"Really? I wasn't aware of that."

"Then the call wasn't referred to her by someone in the office?"

"No. I was the only one here that morning, and I didn't refer anyone."

Sydney frowned. Without a lead, tracking the caller would not be easy. "Do the counselors give out their home phone numbers?"

"They're not supposed to, but there's no way to know for sure. If I had to guess, I would say she probably did on occasion."

"Mr. Ingram, I would like to take a look at Hilary's case files. It's very important that I find the person who called her."

Ingram rubbed his chin. "I don't know. . . ."

"I wouldn't ask if I didn't think it was important."

"Perhaps not, but certainly you must understand about the confidentiality involved. The information in our client files is very personal and of a sensitive nature. These women come to us because they know we won't violate their trust."

"I understand, but you have an obligation to Hilary Walker as well."

"I don't see—"

"What if she responded to a call for help from one of your clients and something happened to her?"

He took a sudden intake of breath. "Oh no," he said, shaking his head. "It can't be. . . ."

91

"I hope I'm wrong, Mr. Ingram, but I have to investigate every possibility. Whoever called Hilary may have been the last person to see her on the day she disappeared."

Ingram continued to shake his head.

"I need to find that person," she said quietly, "I need your help."

Ingram returned to the desk with an armful of folders he had culled from overfull drawers. "Each counselor's files are color coded," he said. "All of the blue folders are Hilary's, and these are her active cases."

The stack was over six inches high and Sydney estimated there were more than thirty folders. "She has quite a caseload."

"Yes. She carried a heavier load than anyone on the staff, myself included." He handed her half of the stack. "You know, Miss Bryant, if you intend to talk to all of these women, you have your work cut out for you; not many of them have phones."

"If I have to I'll visit each one, but what I'm looking for are the women who've had the most frequent contact with Hilary, or anyone who has had a recent crisis. Or anyone with the initials C.T."

"C.T.?"

"According to one of the two appointment books she kept, Hilary had a standing appointment every Tuesday and Thursday at two p.m. with a 'C.T.' "

"Interesting," he said, and opened the top folder. "I can't recall ever hearing her mention anything of the kind. But then, I only worked with her."

Ingram's smile came and went quickly, and then he lowered his eyes, but not before Sydney saw the pain in them.

He cares for her, she thought.

Twenty minutes later they had compiled a list of names and addresses. Two had phone numbers, but both of those were women who seemed to have settled back into the mainstream.

None of the women's initials were C.T.

There were five cases that they judged as active enough and volatile enough to qualify as "possibles." In one instance, Hilary had helped the woman obtain a restraining order against the woman's husband. In another case, there'd been a nasty confrontation with a drunk boyfriend who had somehow located his runaway lover. The man had threatened Hilary with a broken bottle when she showed up with a bag of groceries for her client. After a second visit to the woman's apartment days later, she'd come out to find her tires slashed.

The three other possibilities were women who had long histories of leaving and then going back to their abusive mates. Hilary had been working determinedly with them to break their patterns.

"If any of these women called her, she

93

wouldn't have hesitated." Ingram's expression was pensive. "She'd do whatever she could to help them."

"Would that include ... helping them hide?"

"Yes, I think so."

It had occurred to her that that might be an answer. Hilary might have deliberately gone into hiding to protect one of her clients.

Except, she thought, there were so many elements of the disappearance that just didn't fit with a deliberate act; anyone going underground needed money, a safe place to stay, and a way to get there.

To the best of her knowledge, Hilary had had none of those when she'd vanished.

TWELVE

Just as she was about to make a left turn onto the freeway on-ramp, Sydney noticed the call light flash on her pager.

"Great timing," she said to it, and glanced in the rear-view mirror. There were several cars in the lane behind her and the through traffic passing to her right was moving at a steady rate. No chance to change lanes.

A horn honked and she completed the turn, accelerating smoothly. The power of the Mustang's five-liter engine left the other cars well behind.

She took the first exit and found a pay phone near a gas station. In the service bay two men were putting tires on an old pickup, and the sound of the pneumatic lug wrench drowned out the operator's voice.

"Sydney Bryant," she shouted into the receiver, "I have a call?"

She did not hear the response, but a couple of

minutes later, when the noise had mercifully abated, Richard Walker came on the line.

"I received your message, Miss Bryant. Has something happened?"

"Yes and no." She shielded the phone mouthpiece against the roar of a passing truck. "Although I did speak to Victor Griffith —"

"He's the reporter?"

"Yes." Sydney quickly outlined their meeting, leaving out only the vague warning that had been Griffith's parting shot.

"I see," Walker said when she'd finished. "What do you make of all of this?"

"To be honest, I think he was on a fishing expedition, but it's difficult to determine what he really knows. Or who is giving him his information."

"Information, indeed." He made no attempt to disguise his irritation.

"I would advise you not to talk to him if he shows up again."

"Rest assured, I haven't the slightest intention of talking to *anyone* from the press. Hold on for just a moment, will you, Miss Bryant?"

Walker apparently covered the phone with his hand, but Sydney could hear a British-accented female voice in the background although she couldn't make out the words. The surgery nurse?

"I'm sorry," he said. "The anesthesiologist has finally arrived and I need to consult with him . . . if there's nothing else?"

"Actually, I wanted to ask your permission to

search the house again."

"Search the house?"

For the first time she heard uncertainty in Walker's voice and wondered at its cause. "Yes, as soon as it can be arranged."

"Well, of course, if you think it's necessary. Ah . . . how about later this afternoon? I should be finished here by four."

"Good, I'll see you then."

It was now only one-fifteen; that gave her more than enough time to check out the first of Hilary's Outreach clients.

Nina Munoz lived in a faded pink stucco building in Ocean Beach. There were twelve apartments, six upstairs, six down, which faced each other across a narrow dirt courtyard. A lone eucalyptus grew in the hard-packed soil.

Apartment J was located on the ground floor, left rear. The shades were drawn on the two front windows.

Sydney pressed the doorbell and waited. When no one had answered after a minute, she pulled open the rusted screen door and knocked.

Although she hadn't heard any sounds from inside the apartment, she had a feeling that she was being watched. She knocked again. "Hello?"

The door opened. The woman stayed back in the shadows and looked at her without much interest, waiting passively for her to speak.

"Are you Nina Munoz?"

The woman nodded slowly.

"Mrs. Munoz, my name is Sydney Bryant, and I'd like to ask you a few questions."

"I don't know you," Nina Munoz said. Her voice came as a surprise, well modulated and almost childlike in its sweetness.

"But you do know Hilary Walker. From Outreach."

Another cautious nod.

"Mrs. Walker is missing, and I've been hired to look for her."

"I don't . . . what do you mean?"

"No one has seen her for several days. No one knows where she is. It's important that I find anyone who spoke to her on Monday, before she disappeared."

"But why do you come here?"

"Because, Mrs. Munoz, of your husband."

Nina Munoz stiffened and took a step backwards. "What has Esteban to do with it?"

On the other side of the courtyard, a door opened noisily and a young man wearing black pants and a white t-shirt stepped out. A red bandana was tied around his leg just above his knee. He folded his arms across his thin chest and leaned indolently against the building, watching them.

Sydney gave him a measuring look and then turned pointedly away. "I think it would be best if we talked about this in private," she said, and brought out the photostat of her investigator's license.

The woman glanced at it uneasily and retreated further into the apartment. "Come in."

Inside the window shades kept out most of the daylight, and it took a moment for her eyes to adjust to the darkness. The room was sparsely furnished, the couch and chairs covered with floral-patterned throws, and the carpet was worn through in places, showing the wood floor beneath. Old cooking smells hung in the air, none identifiable.

"Come . . . I have supper to prepare."

They passed through a swinging door into the small kitchen. There was barely room for them both. Sydney sat on a straight-backed chair by an old Admiral refrigerator and watched as the woman moved between sink and stove, slicing vegetables into a pot.

The shade was drawn on the window above the sink, but there was a light on and for the first time she could clearly see Nina Munoz.

In her mid-twenties and very pretty, she wore her thick dark hair gathered in a bun at the nape of her neck. Green, almond-shaped eyes gave her an exotic look. A chipped front tooth was the only imperfection.

"Mrs. Munoz, when did you last see or talk to Hilary Walker?"

"You said this has to do with Esteban?"

"It may have. Three weeks ago, when Mrs. Walker went with you to court to obtain a restraining order against your husband, he became angry."

"Yes." She shrugged. "Always he was angry. About many things."

"According to your file, your husband made

several threatening calls to the Outreach office that same afternoon. Specifically, he threatened Mrs. Walker because she helped you."

"He threatened me, also." She gestured with the knife. "He sent a message through one of his *friends* that a piece of paper makes no difference to him, it means nothing. Less than nothing."

"Has he bothered you since then?"

"I haven't seen him."

"No further messages?"

"No."

"There's been no trouble at all?"

"No. He has always talked of how brave he is, how he fears nothing, but he is only a little man who likes to beat women, and now I have friends of my own."

Sydney wondered whether the young man from across the way was one of them. From the frying pan into the fire? "About Hilary Walker . . ."

"Mrs. Walker is also a friend."

"When did you last see her?"

The young woman's expression became wary again. "I don't know. Maybe on Friday."

"This past Friday?"

"Yes, I think so."

"But you're not sure?"

"It could be Thursday. The days are very much like one another."

"She came by to see you?"

"Yes. Mrs. Walker brought some school clothes for Mary and Jesse."

For some reason, that came as a surprise; she

had seen nothing to indicate that children lived here. "How long did she stay?"

"Just until they came home. To make sure the clothes fit. Two dresses for Mary and a new red coat. For Jesse she brought blue jeans and long-sleeved shirts." Remembering, she let her guard down and smiled. "They have so little . . . they were so happy. Wait . . . it *was* Friday. There was no school the next day . . . no place to go wearing their new clothes."

"You haven't seen or spoken to her since?"

"No." She hesitated, lowering her eyes, but when she looked up the caution was no longer there. "I thought she would come by again, as she promised—"

Sydney interrupted, "When was that?"

"When she left on Friday she said she would come again on Tuesday morning. She had forgotten something at home that she meant to give to Mary. She promised she would bring it by."

"And she never showed up?"

"No."

"Has that ever happened before? Has she ever said she would come and then didn't?"

Nina Munoz shook her head. "Mrs. Walker always said the truth. You tell me she has disappeared—something has maybe happened to her?—but I know it has to be so, because otherwise she would never disappoint my Mary."

"No, I'm sure she wouldn't."

The pot on the stove had begun to boil, and the steam rising from it made the air feel sticky and oppressive. Behind the shade the window

101

was painted shut.

Sydney handed Nina Munoz one of her cards. "Please call me if you remember anything else, anything at all," she said. "And thank you very much for your time."

"Time is one thing I have plenty of."

A group of children were coming up the street toward her. Sydney sat in the car for several minutes, watching them and wondering what had kept Hilary Walker away.

THIRTEEN

The second of Hilary's Outreach clients lived up the coast in Oceanside, but it was getting late and she wouldn't have time to make it there and back before meeting Richard Walker at his home at four o'clock. With less than an hour to kill, she drove instead to downtown La Jolla to the Mon Ami Salon.

Trendy to a fault, the salon actually offered valet parking.

Bemused, Sydney watched the Mustang disappear into the enclosed parking structure. She heard tires squealing and shook her head: there wasn't a valet ever born who could resist the lure of a big engine.

Neither could she.

She crossed to the salon entrance, half expecting to find a doorman or perhaps an armed guard. An electronic eye anticipated her arrival and the door opened, sending forth a fragrant cloud.

The receptionist, an aging blonde with inch-long blood-red fingernails, looked up as she came in.

"Yes? May I help you?"

Sydney heard the doubt in the woman's voice and wondered how it could be that obvious that she didn't belong among the salon's select clientele. Of course, her own hair was "done" as soon as she ran a brush through it.

"I'd like to speak to Philippe," she said, bringing out the photostat of her license.

A pencil-thin eyebrow arched in disapproval. "That isn't possible. He's in the middle of a consultation and can't be disturbed."

Sydney resisted an urge to laugh. "I'm sorry ... I had no way of knowing. In that case, do you have a phone I could use?"

Her expression suggested that it was an imposition, but the receptionist indicated an ivory and gold telephone on the desk. "Please keep it brief."

"Certainly." Sydney picked up the receiver and then hesitated. "Would you happen to know the police department's number?"

The woman started violently. "What?"

"If he's too busy to speak to me, maybe he can find time to talk to the police."

Now the woman looked as though she had picked up a rock and found some slimy, disgusting thing squirming beneath it. "Come with me," she said through her teeth.

Sydney smiled.

The inside of the salon was not at all like the beauty parlors her mother had dragged her to when she was a child. Gone were the assembly-line chairs, the stainless steel shampoo sinks, the glare of the fluorescent lights, and the merciless mirror.

Or if not gone, the workings were at least secreted behind white louvered doors.

Welcome, she thought, to the twentieth century: all civilized societies hide their devices of torture.

Whatever her expectations had been, Philippe was not precious.

Had he been dressed in overalls, he would have looked at home on an Iowa farm. About five-foot-six and sturdy, he was the quintessential country boy, right down to his cornflower-blue eyes and brown hair.

The *artiste* even had a cowlick.

"I'm Philippe," he said, extending a wide-palmed hand.

"Sydney Bryant. Thank you for seeing me."

"A command performance, or so I understand." He led the way into a small lounge and closed the door behind them. "What on earth did you say to get past Tatia? I've never seen her so ... so ... aghast."

105

"I believe I may have implied that if necessary, I would call the police."

"I can see how that would get her attention." He smiled, watching her intently. "A SWAT team might not be intimidated by a withering glance. Was that a bluff or would you have called them?"

"Maybe. The real question is, would they come? That I don't know." She sat on a chair that appeared to have been sculpted out of ice. "I wanted to ask you about Hilary Walker."

"Ah, yes. I was sorry to hear about it. Of course, the rumors are flying, fast and furious. Nasty talk, all the way around."

"Such as?"

"Well, the smart money is on the husband. Talk has it the marriage was over before the ink had even dried on the license. The consensus seems to be that he wanted to cut his losses and save the expense of a divorce settlement. And to avoid the notoriety that comes of airing one's dirty linen in public."

Nasty talk, indeed. "Do you think there's a basis for any of that?"

"Is there ever?" He shrugged. "I don't know. All I can say with any certainty is that in the time I've known Hilary, I've never thought of her as being unhappy. She never seemed dissatisfied with her life. Not like some of the ladies."

"How was she on Monday?"

"Quiet. A little distracted. She sort of stared at her reflection in the mirror, but it wasn't like she was actually seeing herself."

"But not upset?"

"No."

And yet, Sydney thought, Hilary had been reported to have been crying a short time before. "What did you talk about while she was here?"

Philippe frowned and rubbed at his chin. "I was afraid you'd ask me that. I've never understood how anyone could go into court and say that on such-and-such a day they said this and that. So much of what I hear I don't really listen to ... it's just background noise."

"You don't remember anything she said that morning?"

He didn't answer right away, but after a moment he frowned. "Not specifically, no. I wish I could, but when I try, all I come up with is that she didn't say much. And that wasn't unusual, either."

"I see."

"I guess that's part of the problem; nothing was different about that day. You always think you'd recall something if it was important, but then it doesn't *seem* important at the time."

"Memory is a funny thing," she said, more philosophically than she felt. "You remember or you don't. You can't force it."

"I suppose not." He still looked troubled. "Maybe it'll come to me in the middle of the night."

"If it does, I'd like to know." She reached in her jacket pocket and extracted one of her cards. "Call me. The number on the bottom is my service."

"I will."

Sydney glanced at her watch. "Well, I won't keep you any longer."

He got up and walked with her to the door. "You know, you have beautiful hair."

"Thank you."

"The style is . . . interesting. Untamed. Wild."

She smiled. "So I've been told, although not usually in such a nice way."

"I'd be glad to work you into my schedule. Maybe a razor cut. . . ."

"I appreciate the offer, but I doubt if I can afford you."

Philippe shook his head. "No, really. The challenge would be payment enough."

This time she did laugh.

FOURTEEN

Walker had not arrived yet.

Sydney parked next to Hilary Walker's red Mercedes Benz convertible and got out to take a look at it. The car was unlocked and she opened the door on the driver's side.

The interior was white and smelled of leather. She slipped behind the wheel and then leaned forward to reach under the seat. Nothing. She checked beneath the passenger seat, with the same result.

In the glove compartment she found the current registration and proof of insurance, an owner's manual, a gold-plated tire pressure gauge, a mileage and service log, and a road map.

She flipped through the manual, looking for any handwritten notes in the margins or loose sheets of paper tucked between the pages. Zero. In the logbook she glanced over the neat entries but saw nothing unusual among them. The car had last been serviced on January 7: it had cost more than she paid for a month's rent.

The map — which was of California — had not been folded correctly. After making a mental note of which sides were where, she carefully unfolded it.

In the top right corner was a telephone number written in pencil.

It was tedious work examining the map, but, section by section, she checked for any extraneous marks. If she had been a television detective there would have been a circle — maybe in red — to mark the spot. No such luck.

She held it so that the afternoon light would show any erasures. Again there was nothing.

Even so, she tucked the map into her inside jacket pocket. The phone number might turn out to be a dead-end but it was worth a try.

Sydney had just gotten out of the car and closed the door when Richard Walker's Jaguar appeared at the top of the drive.

"Miss Bryant." Walker was dressed smartly in a charcoal-gray suit, blue shirt, and maroon tie. He looked cool, in control, and very prosperous. "I hope you haven't been waiting long."

"It was only ten minutes. I managed to keep myself amused."

"Ethan says you're resourceful."

"It's my Girl Scout training."

His sidelong glance at her was puzzled, but he smiled all the same.

She watched him unlock the front door. He

110

wore a plain gold wedding band, and his hands were strong and slender, with well-shaped fingers. The hands of a healer, a surgeon, a man who saved lives.

Would his training have made him a skillful killer, as well?

"What about you?" she asked, the words out before she realized what she was saying.

"Excuse me?" The front door swung open but neither of them moved.

What the hell, she thought. "Dr. Walker, did you have anything to do with your wife's disappearance?"

For a moment he stared at her, his blue eyes cold with fury. Then he startled her by laughing. "Ethan warned me you had a tendency to be outspoken. But to answer your question: no. I love Hilary. Very much. I would never, *never* do anything to hurt her."

With that, he turned and went into the house.

Sydney followed him. "The reason I ask is because several people have intimated that your marriage is on the rocks."

"Really?" His tone was scathing. "Who are these people?"

"Who they are doesn't matter—"

"It does to me. If people are spreading rumors about me, I want to know."

"The important thing," she said pointedly, "is finding Hilary. To do that, I need to know the truth."

"What is it they say? 'The truth shall make you free.' But I haven't lied to you."

"Someone is lying. I need to find out who."

Walker went to the bar and poured himself a drink. With his back to her he asked, "What are they saying?"

"That you are having an affair." She paused, giving him an opportunity to respond.

He said nothing.

"Dr. Walker, I can't continue my investigation unless you are honest with me."

"Can't or won't?"

"The result is the same. I have to know whether or not Hilary left willingly."

"As you say, Miss Bryant, the result is the same."

Sydney felt a flash of annoyance. "Not so. If she's running, I need to know. And so far, what you've told me about your relationship doesn't quite tally with what I've heard elsewhere."

"Well." He turned and lifted his glass. "To honesty, then." He motioned to her to sit down and did so himself.

"We had an argument Sunday evening, but it isn't what you think. There is no 'other woman.' It might be simpler if there were."

They were sitting on opposite ends of the couch, facing each other, and Sydney felt the full force of his personality as he looked directly into her eyes.

"What did you argue about?"

"Our way of life."

She shook her head; it wasn't what she had expected to hear. "I don't understand."

"Neither do I. But in the last six months or

112

so, Hilary had come to the conclusion that it was wrong for us to live so well."

The result of her work at Outreach? "What did she want to do differently?"

"Everything. She had some fantasy that we should sell the house and join the Peace Corp. She made it very clear to me that she thought I was wasting my talent, and that I could do more good in some backwater country giving tetanus shots and delivering babies."

"You don't agree."

"No. I do more than my share of gratis surgery, and I took a surgical team to Mexico City after the earthquake, but I don't feel obliged to give up everything I've worked so hard for."

Sydney did not comment, but her mind was racing: had Hilary simply walked away from her wealth? Perhaps she'd been unable to reconcile her privileged life style with the poverty she saw around her. It might explain why she had taken nothing with her.

"The point is," Walker said, "the argument wasn't anything new. It wasn't any more heated than any of the other quarrels we'd had on the subject. We didn't even raise our voices."

But who could tell what might prove to be the final straw, the last little thing that made a situation intolerable? A person close to the edge wouldn't need a running jump. . . .

"We made love that night. She slept in my arms."

The shadows in the room had deepened with the coming of dusk, and she could no longer see

113

his expression, but his voice was without warmth.

Outside, a car pulled up, its headlights sweeping across the front windows.

The unmistakable sound of police radio communications brought them to their feet.

Lieutenant Mitchell Travis was accompanied by a uniformed patrolman. Dressed in a dark suit, Mitch looked like anything but what he was: a born cop with the instincts of a street fighter.

The only manifestation of that side of him was the scar on his chin where he'd been kicked while subduing a punk who had freaked out on PCP.

Mitch's hazel eyes met hers and she saw the warning in them: *Stay out of this.*

"Dr. Richard Walker?" He spoke quietly, with the polite hostility that was his trademark.

Walker stepped forward, hands thrust in his pockets. "What can I do for you?"

"I wonder if you'd mind coming down to the station with us."

"Why should I mind?" he said, but she could feel the sudden tension in his stance.

Mitch smiled and nodded. "Good."

As if on cue, the patrolman, who had remained silent in the background, reached to open the back door of the police car.

Walker looked at Sydney. "Call Ethan, will you?" He didn't wait for a reply, but moved past

114

Mitch off the porch.

She watched Walker get into the police car. The patrolman shut the door and went around to the driver's side, then hesitated, glancing in their direction.

"I'll be with you in a second," Mitch called to him, but his eyes did not move from hers.

Sydney waited until she heard the car door close. "What's up?"

"Oh, routine police business."

"Routine."

"We need to clarify a few points of Dr. Walker's statement."

"Correct me if I'm wrong—"

"Don't worry, I will."

She ignored that. "—but I've never heard it called *routine* to pick someone up in a police car just to clarify a statement, particularly when there's no proof that any criminal act has taken place."

"You do amaze me sometimes." He shook his head in wonder. "But I think Ethan Ross is contaminating your mind. I am not here in an adversarial position."

"Wait a minute, let me find my boots, because that's bullshit and it's getting deep fast."

He laughed. "I don't know what you're talking about."

"We both know it's an old police trick, picking someone up at the end of the day when there's a good chance there'll be a delay reaching an attorney."

"What makes you think he needs an attorney?

We're not arresting him."

His smile infuriated her. "He'd be on firmer ground if you were."

"Well, kid," he said, taking a step backwards, "maybe we can arrange that ... and soon."

— FIFTEEN

Sydney went into the kitchen to use the phone. She dialed Ethan's office, pacing as she listened to the line ring. It rang five times and she was about to hang up when he answered.

"Ross here."

"Ethan, I'm glad I caught you."

"I was going out the door."

"The police were just here. They've taken Richard Walker in."

"*What?*"

"They didn't arrest him, but they weren't particularly friendly, either. He asked me to call you."

"Damn. I'd better get down there and run interference. Was it Travis?"

"Who else?"

"Did he say anything? Do you have any idea what he's after?"

"Not really. In fact, he's playing this one extremely close to the vest. Whatever he wants, he's not talking ... at least to me."

Ethan sighed. "That's great."

"Maybe he'll tell you." She tucked the phone against her neck and used both hands to hoist herself up on the kitchen counter. "You were partners."

"So were Martin and Lewis, but you don't see them chumming around."

"They weren't policemen."

"And neither am I, anymore. Listen, I'd better get down there. What about you? Maybe you can charm something out of the lieutenant."

It was a toss-up as to which she liked least: the suggestion or the tone of his voice as he made it. Sydney counted quickly to ten, more slowly to twenty, and decided to ignore both. "I think I can get more done if I stay here and search the house."

"You're at Richard's now?"

"Yes."

"How long will that take? To search, I mean."

"An hour or two."

"I'll call you there when I find out what the official story is. Hell, why don't we go out to dinner afterwards to compare notes? I'll even pay."

"Be still my heart. All right, counselor, you've got a deal."

"Good enough. And Sydney, be careful."

"Of what?"

"When I talked to Richard this afternoon, he told me he's been getting some weird phone calls in the past few days."

She turned to look out the kitchen window. The yard lights had not been turned on and it was now fully dark. "Thanks," she said, "that's just what I needed to hear."

Sydney sat at the small desk in the kitchen office and opened the largest of the three drawers. Walker had said that Hilary handled the household accounts, and most of what she found pertained to that.

The Walkers hired a shopping service to buy groceries and other items, using a computerized order form. Whatever their life style, they at least did not eat extravagantly: Hilary's choices ran to seafood, lean meat, fresh fruits, and vegetables.

They also had employed a cleaning woman who came in twice a week, on Tuesdays and Fridays. The woman's name was Lupe Martinez, and a copy of her green card was filed with the other paperwork.

Sydney copied the name and address into her notebook.

She found the bank records for Hilary's separate personal checking account and verified that there had been no unusual activity – specifically, large withdrawals – in previous months. The balance as of the January 20 statement had been in excess of fifty thousand dollars.

The joint checking account hovered around six hundred thousand dollars. Two savings passbooks showed three hundred and seventy thousand dollars more.

Very liquid assets, she thought.

The credit accounts—American Express, Carte Blanche, MasterCard, plus several cards from the more exclusive stores in the area—showed little activity. Most of the charge slips had been signed by Richard Walker.

One folder marked "utilities" included the telephone bills. She separated the pages listing long distance calls from the others and set them aside to take with her.

In a second drawer she found rubber-banded bundles of correspondence. The thickest bundles were letters from various other Walkers. None lived in California, and in any case, there were no recent postmarks.

Hilary reportedly had no family left, but Sydney belatedly realized that she didn't know Hilary's maiden name.

She made a note to herself to find out.

Most of the envelopes were addressed to Dr. and Mrs. Richard Walker, except for a packet of letters from Mara Drake. Those were written on onionskin paper and mailed from foreign countries.

Sydney opened a letter dated October 6 of the previous year, posted from New Zealand.

Dearest Hilary:

It's the oddest feeling to leave home in the fall—or at least as much of a fall as Southern California can lay claim to—and

120

arrive elsewhere in the spring. Can you imagine? Summer will be here soon.

I wish you would reconsider. Summer is always so kind to you and it would do you good to get away.

If you change your mind, we could rent a house by the ocean and spend long, lazy days walking on the beach.

On The Beach. I loved the movie, and bought the book to read on the flight down. Somehow the world ending didn't seem so bad. . . .

As you might guess, I'm still out of sorts from the jet lag, or maybe I just feel guilty for leaving you to face things on your own. But I will be back, I promise.

And you must promise to wire me if you need anything. It isn't a sign of weakness to need someone, you know.

Take care of yourself.

It was signed, love, Mara.

Sydney tucked the letter back in its envelope and put it back with the others, then sat for a moment thinking.

What "things" had Hilary been facing last October? More important, did whatever it was have anything to do with her disappearance?

The further involved she got in this case, the more questions were raised. Questions whose answers were really only other questions in disguise.

As a ten-year-old, she had taken up the yo-yo. Most of the time she could make it do what she wanted, but every once in a while it seemed to fly from her hands with a purpose of its own. Invariably, the string would become tangled, and she would spend days, sometimes, undoing knots.

This reminded her of that.

Except these knots were holding fast.

After finishing in the kitchen office, she made her way upstairs.

As it had been on Monday, the master bedroom was immaculate. The black lacquered furniture shone in the soft light from the bedside lamps.

Feeling a little foolish, she checked the backs of picture frames and the bottoms of drawers, ran her hands along the underside of the chairs, and flipped through the pages of several medical books.

She was on her knees unscrewing the plate of an electric outlet when the phone rang. Off balance when she reached to answer it, she dropped the receiver on the floor.

"Hello?" she heard a female voice say, "Richard, are you there?"

She pulled at the cord and brought the phone to her ear. "I'm sorry," she said, "Dr. Walker isn't in. . . ."

The line clicked softly and the dial tone began to sound. She frowned as she hung up, reasonably certain that the caller had been the British nurse she'd spoken to that morning.

"You may not want to talk to me," she said aloud, "but I'm *going* to talk to you."

Forty minutes later she finished her search of the bedroom with little to show for the time and effort.

Neither Hilary nor Richard Walker kept any personal papers upstairs. She found no journals, no diaries, no scented love letters or flowers pressed between the pages of a book of poems.

There were no hidden safes, no drawers with false bottoms, nor, she thought fancifully, were there gold coins sewn into the hems of winter clothes.

She did find the gray cable knit sweater that Hilary had worn to lunch on Monday. From that – and the presence of the Mercedes Benz in the driveway – she could assume that Hilary had safely arrived home that afternoon.

Not exactly a break in the case.

After a final look around, Sydney turned out the lights and started down the stairs.

The phone began ringing as she reached the halfway point, and she quickened her pace. She picked it up in the living room, but did not speak. It wasn't as easy to control her breathlessness.

"Sydney?"

"Ethan, yes, it's me."

"What's the heavy breathing for?" He laughed.

"You sound like you're getting ready to make an obscene phone call."

She stuck her tongue out at the phone. "You wish. So, what's the story?"

"They cut him loose a few minutes ago, prompted no doubt by an emergency call from the hospital O.R. They brought him in to – and I quote – clarify a few points of his statement."

"That's what Mitch told me. What points needed clarification?"

"I'll tell you when I see you. Are you about through there?"

"Almost."

"Why don't we meet at The Shores? Say, in half an hour?"

The Shores was a casually stylish restaurant on Camino Del Oro in La Jolla, which featured a spectacular view of ocean and served the best shrimp scampi she'd ever eaten. "I'm really not dressed for it," she said.

"You'll be with me ... who'll notice what your're wearing?"

"One of these days, Ethan ..."

"Then we'll make it an hour, and you can go home and change."

"I'll be there," she said, and hung up the phone.

It rang again as she started out the door.

Maybe Ethan couldn't get reservations, she thought, and went to answer it.

But it was not Ethan.

A voice whispered, "Stay out of it . . . it's none of your affair."

She whirled, aware that she'd left the door ajar and not wanting to have her back to it. "Who is this?" she asked, tightening her hold on the receiver.

"Stay out of it."

Sydney thought she detected a mechanical quality to the voice, as though a synthesizer were being used. "You've watched too many B-movies," she said. "I don't scare that easily."

"And I don't give second warnings."

The line went dead.

SIXTEEN

The light on the apartment landing had burned out and Sydney stood in the dark as she unlocked the door. Something brushed against her legs, and she resisted an impulse to kick out.

The phone call had made her jumpy, after all.

Reaching inside, she found the switch and turned on the lights.

The neighbor's black and white tomcat ran past her into the apartment, heading straight for the kitchen.

"Trouble, get your tail back here." She shut the door, then dropped her shoulder bag on the couch as she went after the cat.

In the kitchen she found him on the counter, sniffing at the cookie jar. She picked up the cat and broke off a piece of a cookie, then put both on the floor. He hunkered down to eat, closing his eyes in contentment.

"You and your sweet tooth. Your mama has to work two jobs just to feed you." She took a cookie for herself – palming it so the cat couldn't

126

see—and went to the bedroom to change.

The windows in her bedroom faced west, and even in February the afternoon sun was strong enough to make the room warm and stuffy by day's end. She opened the window to let in some fresh air, then stood, enjoying the breeze and looking out at the night.

Although the latest weather forecast was calling for scattered thundershowers during the early morning hours, for now the sky was clear enough to see the brightest of the stars. Looking at the stars, she tried to imagine how they would look from far out at sea, away from all of the city lights.

Beautiful, but isolated . . .

As was Hilary Walker?

She thought of the photographs Richard Walker had given her. The first Hilary—the prim and proper one—didn't look as though she were a chance-taker. Regardless of what Walker had said about his wife's dissatisfaction with their life, it was difficult to envision that Hilary turning her back on the wealth and privilege he'd provided.

The other Hilary, however, might be impulsive enough to go off on her own just to stir things up. The second Hilary would not be afraid.

More than any other fact, Sydney needed to know which woman she was looking for.

Sirens wailed in the distance as she backed the Mustang out of the carport.

There'd been a four car accident on La Jolla Village Drive at Torrey Pines Road, and traffic was backed up, moving slowly as the curious looked for signs of carnage. A makeshift lane had been outlined with flares, and a motorcycle cop tried to wave the drivers along, but their eyes were elsewhere.

She was fifteen minutes late getting to the restaurant. The underground parking lot was full and she was lucky to find a space on Vallecitos next to Kellogg Park.

Ethan had apparently been watching for her. He walked up to the car as she got out.

"I thought you stood me up," he said.

"I have to admit it crossed my mind. What I really need is a good night's sleep."

"We can make it an early evening." He offered her his arm and they started toward the entrance. "By the way, you do look great. . . ."

"I tried, but who'll notice?" Sydney smiled. "I'm with you."

Their table was by a window and Sydney looked out at the ocean, watching the moonlight, which seemed to dance across the waves. The storm — wherever it was — had not yet reached the coast.

Ethan raised his glass to her. "Are you sure you don't want a taste of the Chardonnay? It's very good."

"Thank you, no. I'd rather not fall asleep during dinner."

"You're working too hard, Sydney. You need to unwind."

"Unravel is the word, and I want to avoid it if I possibly can. Anyway, you promised to tell me what happened with Richard Walker."

His expression became serious. "Actually, not much. I'm reasonably sure that the police are only sniffing around, though I let them know I consider this particular incident just shy of harassment."

"What are they after?"

"It's hard to tell. They're being very careful about what they say, and our friend Jake was sitting in to make sure they didn't overstep their bounds."

She considered that for a moment and then shook her head. "Are they being careful because of who Walker is, or because they think he's done something and don't want to blow their case?"

"Could be both."

"Have they got anything to go on?"

"I haven't a clue. The legal concept of discovery doesn't exist at this stage of the game."

"What did they ask him?"

"About what you'd expect. What time he arrived home; what he did when he got there; where he'd been — and with whom — earlier that day. And of course, how were they getting along."

"Any surprises?" she asked, thinking of what Walker had told her about the argument they'd had.

Ethan frowned. "Only that Richard was alone in his office from four-thirty on that day."

"Wait a minute. . . ." she began, then fell silent as the waiter approached. The scampi smelled delectable, as always, but she was no longer hungry.

"I know," he said when the waiter left. "It could complicate matters."

"That's putting it mildly." Sydney leaned forward and lowered her voice. "Ethan, what the hell is going on? Did Walker tell you any of this beforehand?"

"No, he didn't. But I don't think he was being evasive or trying to hide anything. And I'm partly at fault, since I didn't ask him where he was. . . ."

Neither had she. "Well, we both should have known the police would ask." She picked up her fork and put it down again. "So . . . where do we stand?"

"On the surface, nothing's really changed. Hilary's disappearance is being investigated as a routine missing person. And, as I said, the police were exceedingly careful talking to Richard. There wasn't even a hint of accusation in either the questions they asked or the way in which they asked them."

"But they *do* suspect him?"

He hesitated and then nodded. "I'd have to say yes. Their presumption is that any time something happens to a married woman, the husband is automatically a suspect. In this case, that basic suspicion is compounded by the fact that Richard is a doctor."

"A doctor without an alibi."

"So it would seem. Apparently he had an emergency surgery that afternoon and his nurse canceled his office appointments. The patient died an hour into the procedure. After that Richard went to the office to catch up on some dictation and was alone there for nearly two hours. He'd checked out on his pager, but he had no calls and saw no one."

"That's odd," she said. "Wouldn't someone have seen him arriving at or leaving the office?"

"He's one of the few doctors who doesn't share a practice, and a couple of years ago he moved his offices out of the medical building. He bought a clinic that had gone out of business and upgraded the facilities to meet his needs. The parking is underground and he uses a private entrance that isn't visible from the street . . . no one could have seen him come or leave."

"God, this is getting complicated. Every time I think I might have a handle on this case, something else comes up. It's as though someone were purposefully muddying the waters. And now . . ." She stopped short. *I'm not going to tell him about the damned phone call.*

Ethan took a sip of his wine. "Then you'd better eat your dinner; you're going to need your strength."

She looked at the shrimp and sighed. "I wonder if cats like garlic?"

Ethan walked her to the car, his arm lightly around her waist.

"Sydney ... tonight Mitch told me he and Carol had separated."

She looked at him. "So I've heard."

"If I know Mitch, he'll be after you to take up where you left off."

"I don't want to even think about that." She felt her face grow warm and was grateful for the cover of darkness. Her relationship with Mitch Travis had been a mistake from the beginning, and she had no intention of seeing him again. That he'd already asked her out was better left unsaid.

"I'm sorry." Ethan took her hands in his and they stood facing each other.

"For what?"

"For a lot of things. For what I said to you earlier on the phone about charming the bastard. Hell, for even introducing you to him in the first place. And not seeing what was happening between you. For not telling you he was married—"

"I figured that out very quickly."

"But not soon enough. You got hurt and I hated to see that. It's one of the reasons he and I don't have anything to say to each other anymore."

"Well, it doesn't matter. You don't have to worry about me, Ethan."

"Mitch can be very persistent when he wants something, and ... he wants you, still. To him, you're the one who got away."

"It doesn't matter what he wants. It's over. . . ."

His eyes searched hers. "Is it?"

"Yes."

"I'm glad. Because I can't help worrying about you. I watched you grow up—"

"Now you sound like my father." She smiled. "You're only eight years older than I am."

"I don't feel like your father. Not at all." He reached to touch her face gently. "Take care of yourself, Sydney."

She covered his hand with her own. "You can count on it."

SEVENTEEN

Instead of going straight home, Sydney decided to drive for a while. She was tired, but she knew from past experience that she wouldn't be able to sleep yet; there were too many things to think about.

Under the right conditions, driving relaxed her and helped clear her mind.

She took Ardath Road to Interstate 5 and headed north. Traffic was relatively light, and she had the fast lane all to herself. After a glance in the rear-view mirror to check for the Highway Patrol, she set the Mustang's cruise control at sixty-five.

The freeway momentarily swelled to eight lanes where the 805 joined, and she again merged to the inside lane. Northbound, the freeway dipped and rose in a gentle swell, an asphalt roller coaster.

Behind her, horns blared furiously and she glimpsed a dark-colored van swerving to pass a slow-moving truck. A second later the van cut off a small foreign car to get over to the fast lane.

She half expected the van either to catch her and speed by or ride her rear bumper, but it stayed several car lengths back.

A tail?

Sydney tapped the accelerator and watched the van's head lights recede. Whoever it was seemed content to let her pull away. When she had tripled the distance between them, she slowed again to sixty-five.

The van's speed remained steady.

Just a bad driver, then.

She allowed her mind to wander.

There were, she thought, so many aspects of Hilary Walker's disappearance that she hadn't worked through yet. The bits of information that she'd collected in two days of investigation were oddly contradictory.

Sydney tried to put an order to what she'd learned so far.

By Walker's own—if reluctant—admission, he and Hilary had argued on the Sunday before she disappeared about her desire to change their lives. Walker contended that the argument was not a new one.

That was unprovable, since Hilary was the only person who could deny or confirm what he said.

And, to some degree, Sydney thought his "admission" extremely self-serving, since it laid the groundwork for a possible explanation as to why Hilary had left without taking anything of value with her.

Walker also had said that he had made love to his wife later that night, which, if it were true, would seem to indicate that, whatever its intensity, the quarrel had not been a "last straw."

Again, though, he could say whatever he wanted. There was no one to refute him.

The following morning, Hilary had been seen crying at the Ladies Club. Rumor there centered on Walker's having an affair. Moreover, Hilary was commonly thought to have known of her husband's infidelity.

Hilary had then gone to her hair stylist, who'd reported she was "quiet," but not distraught. Talk among the salon's clientele also suggested that the Walker marriage was on the brink.

As intriguing as the rumors might be, talk alone was a far cry from hard and fast proof. Walker denied being involved with another woman and insisted his marriage was happy.

Why then had Hilary been crying? There was no way of knowing, no more than there was a simple way of confirming any of what Walker had said.

At lunch, Hilary reportedly had been "fine." Yet Mara Drake had hinted that there had been unspecified problems in the past, and the letter she'd written Hilary from New Zealand tended to substantiate that.

If anyone would know what was on Hilary's

mind, wouldn't it have been her closest friend? Or was she so private a person that she guarded her secrets from everyone?

Arriving home after lunch, Hilary apparently had had an unexpected guest. They'd had a drink together and one of them had been cut by the broken glass. Assuming Hilary was injured, the guest might have taken her to get medical aid. Only none of the hospitals in the area had treated her, or at least, not under her own name.

Other alternatives included the possibility that her caller had been the one hurt. Or that the injury had not required more than a bandaid.

Presumably, the police would have tested the blood found at the scene, but the significance of such testing was in fact minimal. Even the most sophisticated analyses could not give an absolute identification, whether or not Hilary's blood type were known.

Then there was the Outreach factor.

Mara Drake had said that Hilary had gotten a call that had necessitated a trip downtown sometime that morning, most probably between ten-thirty and twelve-fifteen. Whatever the emergency had been, the situation was at least temporarily under control by the time Hilary had arrived at Elario's for lunch.

She *might* have received another call later that afternoon, but if so, how had she responded to it? Obviously, she had not taken her car.

Karl Ingram had indicated that Hilary was a tireless worker who willingly put in the necessary time to do her job. There was little doubt that in an emergency she would have done whatever she could to help.

If she had given out her phone number, might she have also given her address?

If she had not gone to the client, could the client have come to her?

Sydney shook her head in irritation: the questions multiplied exponentially, but the answers were few and far between.

Add to that the new revelation that Richard Walker could not convincingly prove his whereabouts when his wife had disappeared. The police suspected him of *something*, and although they weren't sharing information with her, she knew they seldom chased shadows.

Seen from the point of view of the police, Walker's actions were questionable. Why, after discovering his wife was missing, had his first call been to his attorney?

True, he had hired a private investigator to look for Hilary, but in the police perspective, that might appear to be a smoke screen. It wouldn't be the first time a guilty party had made a show of concern.

Motive, as Ethan had said, was considered strongest for those most intimately involved. With regard to motive, the possibility of Walker's involvement with another woman could not be ignored.

And despite his denials, Sydney could not help but wonder. There were the persistent rumors, of course, and also that phone call from the British nurse.

Which reminded her of the other call, and the anonymous voice warning her off.

She glanced in the rear-view mirror.

The van had closed the gap and was right behind her. She could make out the silhouette of the driver, but the light reflecting on the windshield obscured his face.

Sydney flexed her hands and gripped the stirring wheel, then floored the accelerator. The Mustang responded with a burst of speed that the larger, bulky van could not hope to match.

They had just passed the exit for Oceanside Harbor Drive, the last major exit for eighteen miles. Having driven it hundreds of times, she knew that this stretch of freeway offered few opportunities to lose a tail.

There was a rest area a few miles ahead, then Las Pulgas Road—which seemed to go no-where—and the INS checkpoint and weigh station. Beyond that, Basilone Road offered access to San Onofre State Beach, and then she would be in southern Orange County.

What she needed was a place to get turned around. More important, a place where it would be difficult for the van to follow her.

Here the north- and southbound lanes of Interstate 5 were separated by metal posts that were connected by a thick metal cable. In addition, dense shrubbery grew along the median, which itself varied in width and depth.

There were several turn-outs, designed for use by the police and other emergency vehicles,

139

which allowed a careful U-turn. Signs prohibited their use by motorists. Even if she was inclined to try, the openings were quite narrow, and it would be a trick to make a fast switchback using a turn-out.

On the other hand, there was a wider turn-out at the INS checkpoint. If she could make that one — and catch the van driver by surprise — she had a chance of losing him.

She looked in the mirror.

The van was coming on.

"Time for a driving lesson," she said.

She began moving to the right-hand lane and slowed her speed just slightly.

Let him think he was catching up on his own.

They were nearing the checkpoint station, which was closed at this late hour.

It was difficult to judge distance traveling at high speed, but as she neared the turn-out, she hit the brakes and turned sharply on the wheel.

The car slid sickeningly sideways, across the number two and three lanes. The Mustang's low center of gravity kept it on the road.

When the slide lost momentum, she downshifted and punched the gas again, shooting straight through the turn-out opening. Her tires spun, flinging gravel, but she hung on, steering tight into the turn.

A second later she was southbound. The car's two hundred and twenty-five horsepower could take it from zero to sixty in six seconds, a quarter of a mile in less than fifteen seconds, and had a top-end speed of a hundred forty-nine mph.

The van would not, could not, maneuver well enough to make that tight turn. If he slowed he could have a go at one of the narrower openings, otherwise it was at least two miles to the next exit – Basilone Road.

By then she'd be long gone.

EIGHTEEN

The sensation of spinning out of control brought her instantly awake.

Sydney sat upright and brushed her hair back from her face. Perspiration made her nightshirt cling to her, and the sheets were tangled around her. She reached down, freeing her legs, and got out of bed.

For a moment she just stood there, slightly disoriented by the vividness of the dream, waiting for her heartbeat to steady.

Then she walked slowly toward the bathroom, pulling her nightshirt over her head. The air felt delicious as it dried her skin.

Even better was the sensuous feel of hot water as it cascaded over her body and soothed the dull ache in her muscles. She adjusted the spray to a fine, tingling mist and raised her face to it.

Her eyes closed, she stood beneath the water for a long time. The heat lulled her, and only when the water temperature cooled did she move to get out.

When she stepped from the shower, she felt better than she had in days.

Wrapped in a towel, Sydney walked to the front room. Her jacket and shoulder bag were on the couch where she'd left them, and she retrieved the map she'd taken from Hilary Walker's car.

Although it was probably a long shot, she dialed the phone number she'd found written on the map. As she listened to it ring, she realized that she didn't really expect anyone to answer.

No one did.

What she needed was a way to keep dialing the number at intervals, over and over and over. What she needed was a computer with a phone modem.

Luckily, the solution to that problem lived right next door.

All of fifteen, Nicole Halpern was an absolute genius with computers. Her mother had died when Nicole was six, and her scientist father had tried to fill the void in her young life by bringing her into his own world. As a result, she had grown up feeling at home around technology in general, and in particular she excelled in the programming of computers.

Nicole had always shown an avid interest in Sydney's work, and occasionally helped with some of the more tedious elements of the job. Last year Nicole had developed the software for a computer program that listed, sorted, and compared telephone records.

"Sydney, hi." Nicole smiled shyly and tucked a lock of silky blond hair behind her ear. She was dressed in the white blouse and dark plaid skirt that served as the uniform of the private girls' school she attended.

"I'm glad I caught you," Sydney said. "Do you have a minute?"

"Sure. Come in."

The Halpern apartment resembled a command post of some kind. In the living room there were four computers of varying degrees of sophistication, as equal number of high-speed dot matrix printers, a three-color graphics plotter, and a bank of telephones.

One of the printers was noisily at work.

Nicole, who was pretty without being aware of it, wrinkled her nose and made a funny face. "Why don't we talk in the kitchen? It'll be quieter there, and anyway, I need to finish making my lunch."

Sydney nodded and followed the girl through the hall. The kitchen was quieter, but even here there was evidence of Ted Halpern's compulsion: yet another computer, a drafting table, and stacks of scientific journals.

"I haven't seen you around much lately," Nicole said, setting to work. She spread peanut butter on a slice of whole wheat bread. "You must be on a case."

"Yes, and to be honest, I'm having a time of it. I've been gathering a lot of information, but not much has come of it so far."

"Is there anything I can do?"

"Yes, if you're not too busy with school."

Nicole took a jar of preserves out of the refrigerator and turned, a thoughtful expression on her face. "School is not exactly challenging these days."

"Why is that?"

"Well, for one thing, the new headmistress seems to think that *proper* little ladies shouldn't bother themselves with anything more demanding than observing the rules of etiquette. They're even talking about reviving the debutante ball. Can you *imagine?*"

Sydney laughed at Nicole's indignant look. "I'd heard that the social graces were making a comeback."

"I think it's all a waste of time. Miss Delacourt insists that we attend all sorts of high teas and *soirées* . . . as if any of that'll get me into a good university." She stuck the butter knife into the jar of preserves and rattled it around. "But never mind what she wants . . . I can say I have a headache and be excused. Being ill is so *déclassé.*"

"If you're sure you won't get in trouble."

Nicole shrugged. "I won't, but even if I did, I wouldn't care. I'd much rather help you."

"Great." Sydney pulled out the map, Hilary's two appointment books, and Walker's long distance phone bills. "First I want to get a name to go with this number." She pointed to the number on the map. "I'd keep calling it myself, but I have a full day today."

"No problem. When I get home this afternoon, I'll program the computer to call at ten-minute intervals until I get an answer. I'll pretend to be conducting a survey or something to get the person's name."

"That's the idea. I also need to know if there are any patterns to these calls on the phone bills. And maybe you can match some of them to the names in the appointment books."

Nicole finished making her sandwich, wiped her hands on a dish towel, and came to stand next to Sydney. She took the larger appointment book and turned to the back pages. "It may take a while," she said, "but I'll do it."

"Thanks, Nicole. I owe you one."

The drive to Oceanside was uneventful; no one was tailing her this morning.

Gretchen Elliott lived in a small wood-frame house on a back street. Both the house and the street had seen better days—the paint on the house had grayed and was peeling, and there were two abandoned cars up on blocks at the end of the street.

The property was surrounded by a rusted chain-link fence and the gate screeched as she pushed it open. In the yard the grass had given way to weeds.

"Who is it?" a voice called when she reached

146

the porch. The front door was open, but the screen shielded the speaker from view.

"My name is Sydney Bryant. I'm looking for Gretchen Elliott." She could barely make out someone standing in the shadows inside the house.

"Huh! Well, she's not here. What do you want her for, anyway?"

As Sydney came to the door, the woman stepped forward. She appeared to be in her seventies, but she was not a frail old lady. Dressed in denim trousers and a flannel shirt, she wore her gray hair in a severe, short style, and her skin was as tanned and leathery as a merchant marine's.

"I'm a private investigator and I'd like to talk to her about her caseworker from Outreach, Hilary Walker."

The old woman's eyes were shrewd. "That the lady who's disappeared?"

"Yes it is."

"What makes you think Gretchen would be able to tell you anything about that?"

Sydney hesitated and decided to be candid. "Mrs. Walker got a phone call from one of her clients on Monday before she disappeared; I'm trying to find who called her. I know that Gretchen has been having problems lately—"

"Lately!" She snorted. "All her life, is more like it."

"Are you related?"

"She's my only grandchild, and I tell you, there's been many a time I thanked the Lord there weren't no more of 'em." The old woman pushed open the screen door. "You might as well come in. Gretchen'll be back soon."

"Thank you, Mrs. . . . is it Elliott?"

"It is, but I go by Hazel." She turned to the right and led the way into a tiny room, which apparently was both the dining room and a sewing room. She sat down heavily in a rocker and then picked up an embroidery hoop. "I'd offer you a drink, but it's early, even for me, and I refuse to have coffee or tea in the house."

"That's all right—"

"You want to know what's wrong with this country and I can tell you in two words. Coffee breaks." The sound of the embroidery needle as it punctured the fabric added emphasis to her words. "If American workers are so delicate that they need to rest every couple of hours, they *deserve* to be sucking eggs."

Sydney smiled. "About Gretchen . . ."

The woman's mouth turned down at the corners. "When she was little, she was such a pretty child, but she's never had a lick of sense. I told her not to marry a Southern boy. I warned her he'd give her nothing but trouble. Would she listen to her old Grandma? No."

"But she's filed for divorce, hasn't she?" Hilary had assisted Gretchen in securing low-cost legal counsel in order to divorce her estranged husband, Billy Ray Baker.

"It'll take more than that for her to rid herself of that boy. He's gotten himself used to having a wife to support him. Billy Ray probably

148

doesn't have three working brain cells to his name, but then neither does a leech, and they have no trouble digging in."

"Mrs. Elliott . . . Hazel . . . was there any trouble between them on Monday?"

Hazel Elliott sighed. "There was. Gretchen stopped making the payments on his truck, and I guess the finance company sent someone out to repossess it. Billy Ray was fit to be tied."

"What happened?"

The old woman's hooded eyes glinted with anger. "He batted her around, bloodied her nose, and then threatened to kill her if she didn't get the finance company to return the truck. Of course, I went across to a neighbor's and called the police the minute he showed up. They came and took him away."

"They arrested him?"

"Yes indeed."

"What time was this?"

"Oh, early afternoon, maybe one o'clock."

Sydney thought about that. If Billy Ray Baker was in jail between three and six-thirty, it would effectively eliminate him as a possible suspect. "Is he still in jail?" she asked.

"Ha! I told you Gretchen has no sense; she refused to press charges. The police were disgusted and so was I, but she wouldn't listen to anyone. Even after all that he's put her through, after the beatings and all the misery he's caused her, she says she won't be a party to putting that sorry excuse for a man in jail."

"Do you know what time he was released?"

Hazel Elliot shook her head. "Can't say for sure because I walked out when I saw what Gretchen was up to. But it had to have been fairly soon after he was taken in, because she works afternoons and she worked that day." She snorted again. "Hell, the fool child probably even worked a few hours of overtime so she could make the back payments on that good-for-nothing's truck. Hasn't the sense—"

"Gran . . ."

They both turned at the sound of Gretchen Elliott's voice.

NINETEEN

Gretchen Elliott stood in the doorway, a grocery bag in each arm. She wore a tube top and blue jeans that seemed molded to her boyish hips. Her dark hair was cut in a punk style that didn't fit her round young face.

"What's going on?" she asked. "Are you talking about me?"

Hazel Elliott didn't answer until she had tied off the embroidery floss and bitten through the threads. "You and Billy Ray. This lady here is a private investigator and she has some questions she'd like to ask you about what happened on Monday."

Sydney noticed the pout on the younger woman's lips. She also saw, beneath thick make-up, the fading bruises on the sullen face.

"If you don't mind," Sydney said, showing Gretchen Elliott the photostat of her license.

"If I did mind, would you go away?"

"Gretchen!" Hazel Elliott leaned forward in the rocker. "I won't have you being rude to someone I've invited into my house."

"You can always talk to the police if you prefer," Sydney added.

Gretchen's shoulders slumped. "All right, I'm sorry. What can I say? It's been a rough week. But I'd better get the groceries put away before something melts." She passed between them and was gone.

A moment later the sounds of cupboards opening and closing vigorously left little doubt as to Gretchen's frame of mind.

"She'll calm down," Hazel said. "She doesn't much take to being told what to do — I suppose she gets that from her dad — but give her a minute to cool off and it'll all be forgotten."

"I understand." Sydney glanced toward the kitchen. "It must be very difficult to have your personal life exposed for a stranger's eyes."

"So what do you want to know?" Gretchen squinted and waved at the smoke rising from her cigarette.

They had gone out on the back porch, which was screened from view and shaded by a huge old oak tree. Gretchen sat in an old-fashioned porch swing and tucked her bare feet up under her.

Sydney leaned against the wall. "You've heard that Hilary Walker is missing?"

"Yes."

"I'm trying to find anyone who spoke to her or saw her after three o'clock on Monday. And I've been told that she may have had a call that day from one of her Outreach clients."

"You think *I* called her?"

"I don't know, Gretchen. That's why I'm here, to find out."

Gretchen frowned and took a drag off her cigarette. "Gran told you about what happened with Billy Ray."

"Briefly, yes."

"Well, I did call Mrs. Walker on Monday...."

Sydney felt a surge of excitement but forced herself to remain silent, since she suspected Gretchen Elliott would say more if asked less.

"You see, I knew that they were going to take back his truck. I hadn't made a payment on it since before Christmas. And when the finance company called me at work the Friday before, I told them where they could pick it up." Gretchen gingerly touched her bruised face. "I knew Billy Ray would be mad, but I just can't pay his bills anymore."

Her voice broke and she shook her head mutely. Tears appeared in her eyes and she wiped angrily at them.

"Take your time," Sydney said.

"I tried to tell him." Her hand shook as she raised the cigarette to her mouth. "I tried to warn him, but he didn't believe I'd actually do it. Then I spent the entire weekend jumping at shadows because I didn't know for sure when the finance people would get around to taking the truck . . . but when they did, I knew there'd be trouble."

Gretchen's voice trailed off and she stared moodily off into the distance.

"So you called Hilary Walker," Sydney prompted after several minutes had passed.

"Yeah. I was scared." She lit a second cigarette. "Mrs. Walker told me that I'd done the right thing, that Billy Ray would continue taking advantage of me as long as I let him."

"What time was this?"

"Pardon?"

"What time did you talk to her?"

"Oh. About ten after eight."

That accounted for the morning call. "You have her home phone number?"

Gretchen nodded. "That was another thing I liked about Mrs. Walker; she wasn't supposed to give out her number, but she did, because she really cares. And she never, you know, talks down to me."

"How did she seem when you talked to her?"

"I don't know . . . the same as always, I guess. She told me not to worry, that everything would work out for the best. She said if Billy Ray showed up, I shouldn't argue with him but I should just walk away." Gretchen sighed. "I tried to follow her advice, I really did, but I've got a temper too, and when he started yelling, I yelled right back and that was when he hit me."

"Your grandmother told me you refused to press charges," Sydney said.

Gretchen nibbled on her lower lip and glanced at the back door. "Gran *was* pretty mad about that. But she doesn't know how it is between me and Billy Ray. I mean, I don't like it when he hits me, but I sort of understand. It's because he ain't never going to amount to nothing, and he knows it. Maybe he'd never admit it, but he knows it deep inside. And now I know it too, and he just can't stand that, to see it in my eyes."

"Even so, I would think that a night in jail might have cooled him off."

She laughed as though surprised by the suggestion. "Anybody else, maybe, but not Billy Ray. He's the type to hold a grudge."

"Have you seen him since Monday?"

"Nope."

"Did he ever meet Hilary?"

"No, although he's heard me talk about her a couple of times." Gretchen looked at her with sudden comprehension. "You don't think he had anything to do with Mrs. Walker disappearing. . . ."

"I honestly don't know," Sydney said.

"Shit." The girl's complexion had paled noticeably. "Billy Ray is crazy, and I'm the first one to admit to that, but he wouldn't do anything so stupid."

"Why not?"

"Are you kidding? Mrs. Walker is *rich*. Even an idiot knows you're asking to be miserable if you mess with somebody who's rich."

"I don't know, Gretchen. He might have resented her for interfering."

"Resentment, yeah, but he wouldn't do nothing."

In spite of Gretchen's protestations, Sydney could see the doubt in her eyes. "If he went to confront her, it's possible that things just got out of hand. He has a temper and a history of striking women who make him angry."

"Not women, *me*. I'm the one who made him mad. He wouldn't take it out on anyone else."

Sydney had the distinct impression that, perhaps subconsciously, Gretchen was uncomfortable with the prospect that her estranged husband could be moved to violence by another woman. Was she jealous?

At any rate, it was pointless to argue. "What time was Billy Ray released from custody?" she asked.

"It had to have been after four. I work a four-to-midnight shift at Denny's, and the police hadn't finished with him yet when I left."

That, at least, could be verified.

"Hey," Gretchen said, her eyes wide, "I just know realized that's another thing . . . Billy Ray didn't have his truck! How could he go getting himself into trouble if he didn't have a way to get around?" Her relief was almost palpable.

Sydney decided against listing the obvious alternatives: stealing a car, catching a ride with a friend, or even using public transportation. "Did you talk to him at the police station?"

A little of Gretchen's enthusiasm faded. "No. I don't know why, but after he hits me . . . he can't stand to look at my face. Maybe it's guilt or . . . but no. He wouldn't talk to me, even after I told the police that I wouldn't sign the complaint."

"How about Hilary Walker? Did you talk to her again that afternoon?"

"No." She averted her eyes.

"Are you certain? It strikes me as odd, Gretchen, that you'd call her at home rather early in the morning because you were scared, and then not call her back to let her know how things turned out."

Gretchen shook her head but didn't speak.

"You told me yourself she really cared about you . . . didn't you think she'd be worried?"

"I suppose." Gretchen reached for a cigarette and busied herself with lighting it.

"What aren't you telling me?" Sydney persisted.

"Not what you think." The sullen pout was back with a vengeance.

"How do you know what I think?"

"I can imagine."

Sydney let the silence lengthen.

"All right, if you must know, I was embarrassed. Ashamed. I didn't want her to know that I'd . . . I'd let Billy Ray off the hook again. Gran and the police, they all looked at me like I was the crazy one. I didn't want her . . . to think so, too."

"From what I've learned about Hilary Walker, I don't believe she would have thought anything of the kind. She was probably genuinely concerned . . . I doubt if she'd have judged you. If anything, I would expect her to be sympathetic."

Gretchen's lower lip quivered and the tears reappeared. This time she did nothing to check them as they ran down her cheeks.

"You're right," she whispered. "Mrs. Walker would've been on my side. I really liked her a lot. I could tell she understood how I felt. The very first time I talked to her, I could see that she knew, that she'd been through it."

Sydney moved to the porch swing and sat on her heels in front of the girl. "Been through what, Gretchen?"

"Someone had hurt her . . . the way he hurts me."

TWENTY

It took only a single phone call to verify that Billy Ray Baker had been released at five-fifteen Monday afternoon without being charged for assaulting Gretchen Elliott.

Sydney thanked the police department records clerk and hung up.

To all extents and purposes, that eliminated Baker from further investigation. The hour and fifteen minutes between his release from custody and the time Richard Walker had had arrived home to find Hilary missing would seem to be cutting it too close.

Assuming Baker had access to a car—and there was no proof that he had—the drive from Oceanside to La Jolla would have taken a minimum of forty-five minutes in afternoon traffic. And there was nothing to indicate that Baker even knew where the Walkers lived.

Then, as Gretchen had implied, even if he had resented Hilary's supposed involvement in the

159

break-up of his marriage, would he have had the nerve to confront her in person?

Unlikely. That would be the equivalent of jumping from the frying pan into the fire.

Sydney walked across the shopping center parking lot to her car and then realized that she'd forgotten to check in with her answering service. When she turned to go back, she saw that someone else was using the pay phone.

"The hell with it," she said. She'd call later from the office. The morning was half over, and she still had a lot to do.

The third of Hilary's crisis clients lived in east San Diego in one of the city's poorest neighborhoods. While there had been a concerted effort between the community and the police to take back the streets from the drug dealers and users, it was a dangerous area for a woman alone.

It was there that Hilary had been threatened with a broken bottle, and where her tires had later been slashed, both acts taking place in broad daylight and in plain view of several witnesses who afterwards could not recall what they had seen.

Although she seldom carried her Smith and Wesson .38 Special, today Sydney had made an exception.

The apartment building where Annabelle Swann lived looked as though it should have been condemned.

Holes had been punched in the stucco, giving it a pockmarked appearance, and all of the exterior trim had been torn away. There were cracks in several of the windows, and someone had used silver duct tape to keep the glass from falling out of the frames.

The staircase that led to the second floor sagged alarmingly along the left side. When Sydney stepped on it, the wood felt spongy, as if it had rotted.

Several children sat on the front steps of one of the ground-floor apartments, and they watched her in silence as she went up the stairs. A girl who looked to be about eight, but whose eyes were much older, held a runny-nosed toddler on her lap.

From somewhere a radio played an old Chuck Berry song.

Sydney found number sixteen without difficulty and knocked on the door. About three feet up from the base of the door was an indentation in the shape of a shoe where someone—presumably the drunken boyfriend—had kicked it open.

She heard a noise from inside the apartment, followed by the sound of several locks and chains being undone. The door stuck in the jamb and had to be pulled open forcefully.

The face that looked out at her belonged to a girl no older than sixteen. She was a light-complected black, but she had dyed her hair blond, and her eyes were ringed with bright blue eyeliner. She wore shorts and an oversized t-shirt proclaiming loyalty to the San Diego Chargers.

"What do you want?" the girl asked.

"I'd like to talk to Annabelle Swann."

"That's me."

Sydney brought out her investigator's license and let the girl study it for a moment. In turn, she studied the girl.

The Outreach file indicated that Annabelle had two children; a boy who had just turned three years old, and a seven-month-old baby girl. The financial assistance she received from the state was her sole means of support.

"Huh, an *investigator*," Annabelle said. "What do you want with me?"

"I have a few questions about what happened a couple of weeks ago ... when Hilary Walker came to see you."

Annabelle blinked. "Oh, that. I'd about forgot about that. Wasn't no big deal. That kinda thing happens around this neighborhood all the time. The police don't hardly bother themselves to come out anymore, unless there's a shooting."

"Can you tell me what happened?"

Her expression was sly. "Seems you'd know, if that's what you come for."

"I'll like to hear it from you."

"Well ... I don't have a lot of time to be wasting ... I got things to do ... I got to get over to the free clinic and get my baby's shots. It's a long walk, what with the two of them to watch after."

"I'd be glad to drive you," Sydney offered.

162

"Would you? Well, I maybe could tell you a few things." She looked past Sydney, her eyes darting back and forth, as though checking to see if anyone was watching. "You might as well come in . . . there's flies enough in here without leaving the door hanging open all day."

The apartment smelled of urine, but more strongly of alcohol sweated during long, hopeless nights. Annabelle swayed slightly as she walked through the small living room and flopped on the couch.

A glass containing clear liquid sat on a watermarked table and the girl reached for it while keeping her attention fixed on Sydney. She raised the glass in a mock salute and then took a drink.

"This is all that keeps me sane," Annabelle said. "Lots of crazy people out there." She gestured toward the window with her glass.

"Tell me what happened. . . ."

"Oh, right. Well, you know, it's just Lionel, the way he is."

"Lionel?" The report she'd read of the incident hadn't mentioned the boyfriend by name.

"Lionel Dean. He's Rainbow's daddy. Rainbow is my baby girl."

"That's a pretty name."

Annabelle shrugged. "It's better than what Lionel wanted to call her . . . Shamika. Like she belongs to a tribe in Africa or something." She wiped at a smear on the rim of the glass with her thumb. "Anyway, what I was saying, is Lionel can get mean now and again, if somebody

163

makes him mad."

"What was he mad about?"

"Save some time, honey, and ask what he *wasn't* mad about. He wanted to marry me, but I said no. Can't take no cut in my benefits, you understand. Then he wanted me to bring the baby and stay at his mother's. Man's crazy if he thinks I'm gonna live in another woman's house again . . . I don't get along with my own mother, so why would I get along with his? Anyway, I told him no. And then he told me to forget going to night school and getting my diploma. I'm still going." She chuckled. "You could say the man was getting *frustrated*."

Annabelle made it sound like a game, but being menaced with a broken bottle was deadly serious. "You think he was taking his frustrations out when he threatened Mrs. Walker?" Sydney asked, barely containing her disbelief.

"Don't know 'bout that." Annabelle downed the last of her drink. "You know the machines they got down at the laundrymat? If you put too much stuff in or even just the wrong *kind* of stuff in—tennis shoes and such—the machine starts thumping and jumping until you think it's gonna come apart, and there's a little light goes on that says 'unbalanced load.' Well, that's Lionel, right down to the bone . . . when he's got too much to think on, he gets a little unbalanced, and he just can't stop himself from making noise."

"He did more than make noise," Sydney noted.

"Yeah, but that was nothing compared to

what he could have done. Anyway, *she* wasn't afraid of him. He sliced her tires and she walked right up to him in front of everybody, and she told him to get out of her face."

That was either very brave or very foolish, Sydney thought. "What did Lionel say to that?"

"Oh, some bully-shit that he'd do what he damn well wanted, and that the next time he did any cutting, there'd be more than dirt on his blade. But you can see ... he ain't hanging around here no more." Making no attempt to disguise the satisfaction in her voice, Annabelle sounded even younger than she looked.

"You haven't seen him in how long?"

"Since that day, maybe two weeks ago. Last time I saw him, he was standing on the other side of the street like this—" she stood up and folded her arms defiantly across her chest, "—talking to some guy in a white Camaro."

"He hasn't bothered you at all?"

"No. And he'd better not, 'cause I got a *new* boyfriend now."

For the first time, Sydney noticed the fullness of the girl's belly.

Annabelle patted her tummy and smiled. "You noticed, huh? I'm only three months gone, but each time I show earlier. That's another reason I'm glad Lionel's staying away ... I don't need him making trouble about this baby."

"Is he ... ?"

"Yeah, it's his." She reached down for her empty glass and started toward the tiny kitchenette. "My mouth's getting dry from all this

165

talking. You want anything to drink?"

"Thanks, no." Sydney thought of all the reports she'd heard over the years about the effect of alcohol on fetal development, but knew it was not her place to lecture the girl. Instead, she asked, "Do you know where I could find Lionel?"

Annabelle turned, her eyes wide with surprise. "Why you want to go and do that? Ain't you been listening? The man is trouble, and you being an *investi*gator won't carry no weight with him. He doesn't feel kindly toward the law, you understand?"

"Did you know that Hilary Walker has been missing since Monday?" At the girl's nod, she said quietly, "I'd like to ask him about that."

"What you be asking for is trouble."

"Do you know where I can find him?"

Annabelle moved behind the counter and opened the refrigerator. "His mama might know," she said. "They pretty close from what he was always telling me." She poured wine from a jug into her glass, spilling some of it.

"Do you have her address?"

She hesitated, an uneasy look on her face. "Or there's a couple of places he likes to hang out. . . ." her voice trailed off and she frowned.

"If I find him, I won't tell him I spoke to you," Sydney said.

"Maybe not, but he'll know. Mrs. Walker would never have been here if it wasn't for me. You ask about her and he knows I'm in it for sure."

"Annabelle, I understand how you feel, but Hilary Walker might be in serious trouble.

Lionel was able to find you even with the shelter helping you hide; I'm reasonably sure he could have found out where Mrs. Walker lived as well. From what you've told me, he even made a threat on her life."

"He's *always* threatening somebody . . . I told you, that's the way he is."

"But sometimes he does what he says he's going to do. He's beat you, hasn't he? You're scared of him."

Annabelle shook her head. "That's different, him hitting me. We got a relationship. . . ."

The girl's strong sense of denial surprised her, although she'd seen the same thing in Gretchen Elliott. "She helped *you*, Annabelle, when *you* needed help."

The girl remained silent.

"I'm going to have to tell the police about this, and they're going to ask you what you know. You'll have to tell them, and I wish you'd tell me."

"Shit." She sniffed the wine and then drained the glass, closing her eyes as she did. "You think if I *co*-operate, maybe the cops will show up the next time that fool's trying to kick down my door?"

They walked to where Sydney had parked the car, Annabelle holding on to her little boy's hand and carrying the baby on her hip.

Cat calls greeted them at the corner where a group of young blacks were lounging near the doors of a market. A sign in the market window advertised tomatoes at thirty-nine cents a pound.

"Hey Annabelle, you still trying to sell your ugly ass? I give you a nickel for it."

Annabelle stopped and stared straight at them. "Can't you see I got my kids here? What's a matter with you? Don't you got no respect for motherhood?"

The obvious leader of the bunch stepped forward. "I got something you can respect, little mama, if you promise not to bite."

Sydney unlocked the car and helped the three-year-old into the back seat. "Come on, Annabelle," she said.

Annabelle flounced around to the passenger side and got in with a show of leg. Glancing at her, Sydney could see the pleasure on her young face.

"Those boys is trash," Annabelle said disdainfully, but as they drove away, she peeked back over her shoulder and laughed.

"Annabelle, I almost forgot to ask you," Sydney said as they pulled up in front of the clinic, "When did you last talk to Mrs. Walker?"

"Oh, that's easy. It was on the first of the month, I called her 'cause my check wasn't in the mail and she told me if ever that happened, she would give me the money to hold me over, you know, until it came."

"Did she?"

Annabelle noded as she lifted the baby up to her shoulder. "Brought it by herself that same day. Gave me a hundred dollars." She pushed open the car door and got out, then held the seat forward to help the boy out.

"I see. Well, thank you, Annabelle, you've helped me a lot."

The girl leaned down to look into the car. "I don't know 'bout that, but I hope you find her, and it ain't just because of the money she gives me, either. She's a good-hearted lady ... I hate to think something bad happened to her after all the nice things she's done."

TWENTY-ONE

Sydney watched the three of them disappear into the free clinic, but her thoughts were elsewhere.

What she'd told Annabelle Swann was true: she was going to give the police Lionel Dean's name. But she also would try to find him herself.

She glanced at her notepad to check the address Annabelle had given her for Dean's mother and then looked in the rear-view mirror before pulling back out in the street.

Her foot remained on the brake. She'd picked up a tail again; the van from last night was parked along the curb about a hundred yards back. Sunlight reflecting on the windshield made it impossible to see the driver's face.

"Damn it," she said, "I haven't got time to

waste on fun and games." She studied the flow of traffic. Several stoplights back she saw what she needed, two large trucks driving side by side. If they stayed in tandem, she could pull out in front of them, using their bulk to hide her car from the van driver's sight.

Luck was with her. The trucks lumbered along, slowing everything behind them. As they passed the van she gunned the engine, her tires squealing as she swerved into the road mere feet in front of them.

Her own rear view was blocked, so she couldn't see what the van driver did in response to her tactic, but when she found the freeway ramp several minutes later after a series of turns, he was no longer following her.

Mitch Travis was at lunch when she finally found a pay phone that worked, so she gave the information on Lionel Dean to the officer on duty.

"If Lieutenant Travis has any questions, he can reach me at my office after two." That would give her an hour and a half to talk to the mother and get back to University City. "Tell him it's important that I talk to him today," she added.

"After two. I'll tell him."

"Thanks." She hung up. The phone was located outside a convenience store and she went in to grab a Pepsi.

To compete with fast food restaurants, the store offered various sandwiches that could be heated in their microwave oven, but although she was hungry, she hadn't time even for that. She grabbed two ice-cold cans from the cooler and carried them to the register.

As soon as she left the store, she popped open the first can, and drank as she walked back to her car.

Lionel Dean's mother lived in one of only two houses on a street lined with apartments.

The house was almost hidden in the shadows cast by the taller buildings on either side, and even more by its distance from the street. It sat at the very back of the lot, seeming to huddle among the bushes.

Sydney followed the white rock pathway to the front door.

"Ain't nobody home," a voice called as she raised her hand to knock. Turning, she saw an old man leaning on a rake near the right corner of the house. The shadows had hidden him, too.

"Does Lionel Dean live here?" she asked.

The old man shook his head. "Nope."

"But it is his mother's house?"

"Hers and the bank's. Mostly the bank's." He stepped forward and wiped his brow with his forearm. "Lionel comes by when he needs something."

"Has he been by lately? Say, in the past two

weeks?"

"Maybe." His glance at her was shrewd. "Who is it wants to know?"

"My name is Sydney Bryant and I'm a private investigator." She offered him her hand. "And you are?"

"Josiah Alexander. A neighbor for many years and a friend of the family." His handshake was as firm and uncompromising as the look in his eyes.

"Mr. Dean may be a witness in a case I'm handling."

"A witness? Well, that'd be a first."

Sydney sensed the irony in his words. "*Has* he been around this week?"

"I think you'd better ask his mama about that."

She smiled: he was very good at avoiding answering questions. "When will she be home?"

"She's usually home by four, but don't hold me to that. Sometimes she works late."

"Is there any way I can reach her before then?"

"I wouldn't be easy. She works for one of those temporary help agencies . . . some weeks she's at a different company every other day."

"Do you know which agency she works for?"

"I'm afraid I don't. You'd best try again after four or so." He leaned down and plucked a weed from the ground. "Damn weeds. Grass you got to water and tend and look after to make it grow, seeing that this land's only desert once removed, but the damn weeds'll sprout if you spit in the dust."

He threw the weed on a small pile that had been raked up and turned to walk away.

"Mr. Alexander . . ."

"Josiah." He didn't stop.

Sydney followed after him and caught up. "Josiah . . . why do I get the feeling that there's a lot you could tell me about Lionel Dean if you wanted to?"

"Probably because it's true."

They passed around the corner of the house to where a rusted wheelbarrow sat full of leaves and grass. A pair of work gloves lay over the hand grip, and the old man began to pull them on.

"I understand your loyalty to Mrs. Dean—"

"How old are you, young lady?" he interrupted.

"Thirty-one."

"I was living here in this neighborhood before you were born." He nodded toward a small house directly across the street. "I've lived in that house for forty-five years, to be exact. Back then, there weren't no apartments around. You got to know your neighbors because they didn't come and go the way these, these . . . *nomads* do."

His words were angry, but she thought the feelings behind them were based on his disappointment—and even loneliness—that his old neighborhood had gone.

"Friendship born of long acquaintance meant something then and it still does, to me if no one else. Now, I've known Lizbeth Dean since she moved in back when Lionel was still just a high-spirited boy. I've seen her through some tough times with him, I don't deny that, but I won't be telling any tales out of school." He sighed. "The woman's had enough heartache without me adding to it."

Sydney listened, watching his face as he spoke, and realized that he was sincere. But as much as she admired his loyalty, there was Hilary to consider.

"I do understand," she said. "And normally I would thank you for your time and try to get the information I need in another way. But I'm working *against* time, and any delay could be deadly."

The old man's shoulders stiffened visibly. "What do you mean?"

There was, she saw, nothing to be gained by holding back. "Lionel Dean made a threat on a woman's life a couple of weeks ago. The woman has since disappeared. The police have his name, and they're looking for him, but you know this is a big city."

Josiah nodded grimly, but didn't speak.

"If he *is* intentionally hiding, he could be anywhere," Sydney continued. "He might have crossed into Mexico. It could take months to find him."

"Who is this woman?"

175

"Her name is Hilary Walker. She'd been helping Annabelle Swann, Lionel's girl friend, and he apparently didn't appreciate her efforts. Mrs. Walker has been missing since Monday afternoon."

For the first time, the old man looked uncertain. "Monday?"

"If you know anything at all that might help me find him. . . ."

But he said nothing, his mouth drawn into a frown. He bent down and took hold of the wheelbarrow grips, then began pushing it across the uneven ground. Each time he hit a bump, small puffs of dirt were released into the air.

Sydney watched him maneuver across the yard. At the curb he paused and looked back at her.

"Lizbeth Dean is a fine woman."

He had spoken quietly, but she heard the determination in his voice. He crossed the street to his own house, left the wheelbarrow in the drive, and went inside.

She left one of her business cards stuck in the front door of the Dean house.

Heartache, she thought, getting into the car. There was more than enough of it to go around, and yet some people seemed to get more than their share.

Even fine women, regrettably.

It was nearing one-thirty. She started the car

and made a U-turn, heading back toward the freeway and her office.

Maybe Mitch would have worked a little magic and found Lionel. If not, she had the names of two bars where Mr. Dean liked to hang out.

TWENTY-TWO

While waiting for Mitch to call, Sydney caught up on her work in the office. She spent half an hour writing reports on the morning's interviews, then sorted through her mail. There were several checks, including one from a former client whom she'd sincerely doubted would ever pay.

Richard Walker had also sent a check. His note instructed her to advise him when she required "additional funds."

The note did not mention Hilary.

Sydney frowned. She found it more and more difficult to understand Dr. Walker. Perhaps he was burying himself in work to keep from brooding about his wife's disappearance, but it seemed to her that he was deliberately maintaining his distance from what was happening.

But then, Ethan had implied that Walker was good at compartmentalizing his wife. Walker himself had told her that he and Hilary led separate lives.

Her first impression of him had been that he was a cold man whose nature didn't allow for intimacy, even with his own wife. She wasn't sure she believed him when he said he loved Hilary. Those pale blue eyes of his had held no warmth.

Could any woman love such a man?

She wondered, *did* Hilary love him? What if Hilary wasn't running *from* a failed marriage, but *to* another man? What if . . .

"Enough," Sydney said, getting up from the desk. She hadn't time to waste on aimless speculation. And for now, at least, her suspicions had no more substance than smoke in the wind.

The phone rang as she started to eat the turkey sandwich she'd ordered from the neighboring deli.

"Bryant Investigations."

"Sydney . . . I understand you want to talk to me."

"Just back from lunch? You're not an easy man to reach, lieutenant."

"I try to be. What can I do for you?"

"Have you made any progress on finding Lionel Dean?"

"We're working on it. How on earth did you come up with him?"

She told him briefly about Dean's threat. "I thought he was worth a look," she concluded.

"Well, we're looking, I can guarantee that. He's a nasty customer. His sheet dates back to eighty-one, when he turned eighteen. And judging by this, he probably had a notable record as a juvenile, when he was still a punk in training."

"What's his specialty?"

"The man's a jack of all trades. A little robbery, a few burglaries, assault, drunk and disorderly, possession of controlled substances ... the list goes on."

Sydney didn't like the sound of that. "Have you a current address on him?"

"Hmm."

"Mitch ... don't forget I *gave* him to you. What've you turned up?"

"You did the right thing, kid. This isn't a guy who's going to sit still for questions unless he sees some muscle. We've got the muscle."

"Damn it then, don't make me sorry I did the right thing."

"Listen, I really can't talk about this now."

Sydney closed her eyes and resisted an impulse to slam down the phone. "If this is going to be a one-way street, where I tell you everything and you play the strong, silent cop, I won't be quite so conscientious about keeping you informed."

"Temper, temper! Don't let yourself get worked up over it."

"That's easy for you to say. You're not the one being stonewalled."

"Sydney..."

The tone he used—his voice of reason—annoyed her further. "Maybe I'm wrong, but I thought we were on the same side. I realize you aren't obligated to tell me anything you don't want to, but it seems to me that we'd both be better off with a little more honesty. Who the hell is stepping on this case?"

"What can I say? You know I can't answer that. Not here and now. But if you want to talk, let's meet somewhere and talk, off the record."

She hesitated. "This isn't another game?"

"You know me better than that."

"I thought I did."

"Come on, Sydney...."

Curiosity got the better of her. "All right, but on neutral ground."

He laughed. "Is there any other kind?"

Sydney knew there were feelings left between them, and Mitch was well aware of it, too, but she didn't want him to think she was afraid to see him.

They arranged to meet at Mt. Soledad.

Sydney turned into the unpaved parking area where Mitch waited beside his car. Hands in his pockets, he walked toward her as she brought the Mustang to a stop.

As usual this high up, the wind blew briskly, and it tugged at the car door as she got out. Mitch was windblown, his black hair tousled like that of a small boy waking from a nap.

There was nothing boyish about the look he gave her.

"Hello, Mitch," she said, brushing her own hair back from her face.

"Come on, let's take in the view."

181

The view was, in fact, breathtaking. They could see La Jolla: the city, its beaches, the cove. Up the coast at Torrey Pines, hang-gliders soared their brilliantly colored wind craft out over the ocean, before circling to land on the sand.

They walked along a narrow trail that led down the slope of the hill until they came to a level spot. For a moment they stood in silence. Sydney took a deep breath of the clear, fresh air, lifting her face to the sun.

"You shouldn't do that, you know."

"Do what?" She glanced sideways at him.

"Look so tempting."

"Mitch—"

"I know what you're going to say." He smiled ruefully. "I promise to behave."

Sydney was all at once aware of how close he stood, and her breath caught in her throat. She moved away from him, trying to make it appear casual, as though she were totally oblivious of his proximity.

"Tell me," she said, "why you suggested we meet."

"That should be rather evident. I wanted to see you—"

"I thought you said no more games?"

"Let me finish. I wanted to explain about what's been happening with Walker."

She met his eyes. "Off the record?"

"Definitely off the record. Otherwise I'd be committing departmental suicide."

"Why are you doing this?" Even though she

had been angry with him for withholding information, it was unsettling to have him suddenly reverse direction.

"You mean, risking my neck, careerwise?"

Sydney nodded. "I've never known you to put anything before the job."

Mitch shrugged and ran his hand through his hair. "Maybe I have a subconscious desire to put it all on the line. Walk that fine edge."

She could believe that about him, but there was something more in those hazel eyes, something she hadn't seen before.

"Or . . . maybe I've changed."

"Don't," she said, knowing that he was no longer talking about his job. "Now is not the time."

"Sydney." He reached out and tucked a strand of hair behind her ear. "Will there *be* a time, or am I out of the running?"

"It isn't a race." What was she saying? Why didn't she stop him before. . . .

His fingers traced her jawline and he lifted her chin. "Can't you love me just a little bit?" His eyes searched hers.

She was holding her breath, expecting him to lean down and kiss her, but instead he merely smiled. He dropped his hand and kept his distance.

A second later she knew why: a group of tourists clamored down the hill past them. One of their number grinned foolishly at her, and she was grateful for Mitch's tact.

Why hadn't she heard them approach?

183

Because, she told herself sternly, *you let him get to you again.*

"Wait a minute," she said, more to herself than to him. "I think we'd better stick to business. What can you tell me about the Walker case?"

"Ah, yes. Well, as I said the other day, the word is this one could be messy. Apparently someone – nobody is naming names – has it in for the good doctor, and this person has managed to persuade the district attorney's office to ride shotgun on our investigation."

"You have no idea who this 'someone' is?"

"No. But whoever it is definitely has an in with the big boys."

Sydney thought of Mara Drake's comment about making enemies and wondered whom Richard Walker had crossed. "How is the investigation proceeding?"

"Slowly. We checked the neighbors on both sides and across the street, but no one could remember seeing or hearing anything out of the ordinary that afternoon. They had very little to say about the Walkers ... they didn't see much of him, and she was considered pleasant enough, but there wasn't a lot of contact between neighbors."

Which didn't surprise her. "What about the glasses in the sink? And the blood."

Mitch shook his head. "There were no usable prints on those glasses, nor was there residue inside them to show what they'd contained. Most of the blood had dried before the lab boys got to it, but they did find a thick drop or two that was still wet enough to test."

"So?"

"They were able to determine that it's Hilary Walker's blood type."

She had expected that as well.

"But," he went on, "there wasn't much of it. Only what you saw in the sink, on the floor and that doorknob. None at all in the sink trap. It could be that she simply cut her hand on the glass when it broke—"

"Why would she go outside, though? She was still bleeding when she left the house. Why not go to the bathroom and bandage the cut?"

"You've got me. Unless she was in a hurry for some reason."

Sydney looked down at her hands. "She was right-handed, and it was probably her right hand that she cut ... doing dishes you hold with your left and wash with the right. So she cuts herself and then uses that hand to open the back door? Why would she do that? It had to have hurt. And where did she go from there?"

"All good questions, but I have no answers for you. For all we know, she vanished the moment she stepped outside the house."

"Wonderful."

"What can I say? I'm not Columbo. The fact is, there's not much to go on. Except..."

"Except what?"

"Walker himself."

"You really think he did something to his wife? If so, what about Lionel Dean?"

Mitch sighed. "Dean muddies up the waters,

I'll admit, but maybe it was both of them."

Incredulous, she could only stare at him and wait for him to go on.

"I'm not suggesting they conspired to do away with the little woman, but maybe Hilary told Walker about the incident with Dean, and he saw it as an opportunity to cast the blame elsewhere."

"God, what an imagination." She shook her head. "If Walker had planned this, don't you think he'd have mentioned it? That his wife was threatened?"

"I think he hired you to find that out."

"Here we go again—"

"I know it's hard to swallow, but stranger things have happened."

"I can't imagine what."

"At any rate, it's Walker we're watching. We'll check the Dean angle out, but what has he got to gain by going after Hilary Walker?"

"What did he have to gain from any of his priors? A little folding money and the unwanted attentions of the boys in blue?"

Mitch smiled. "Good point. Anyway, we're hot on his trail. I've sent a couple of cars over to check on his hangouts."

"You *will* let me know if you pick him up?" She decided it was better not to mention that she would continue looking for Dean herself.

"Sure."

In other words, she thought: maybe. "I would appreciate it," she said.

"Well, I'd better be getting back." He made no

move to leave, but stood very still, his eyes on hers. "It's been nice seeing you ... I'm glad we could talk."

"We could always talk, Mitch," she said quietly. Then, before he said anything more, she turned and started back up the hill.

TWENTY-THREE

Since the police were going to check the bars Lionel Dean frequented, there was no need for her to do the same, at least for the time being.

If Dean was at one of his favorite hangouts, the police would pick him up; if he wasn't, the word that the cops were inquiring after him would get around and he would know to stay away. He might go further underground.

And his mother, her best hope for finding him, would not yet be home from work.

Sydney felt oddly restless.

It wasn't as though she had nothing to do. There were still two more of Hilary's Outreach clients to talk to; she hadn't had a chance to question Lupe Martinez, the Walkers' maid; and she also wanted to try to find the British nurse who had called Richard Walker the night before.

Which to do first?

The hospital was closest. By the time she'd finished there, it would be after four and she could go again to see Lizbeth Dean.

In spite of what Mitch had said, she had a strong feeling about Lionel Dean.

Or was that wishful thinking on her part?

Sydney arrived at the hospital at three-thirty, the change of shift for nurses working the traditional day hours. It hadn't occurred to her before, but as she walked through the hall toward Surgery, she hoped the British nurse had not gone off duty.

One of her friends from high school had gone into nursing, and she knew that ten- and twelve-hour shifts were not uncommon in a profession that seemed always in the midst of a shortage.

Maybe she'd get lucky, and find the nurse after all.

"I'm sorry . . . who are you looking for?" The nurse was dressed in scrubs, and a surgical mask hung from around her neck.

"I don't know her name, but she has a British accent. I've only talked to her on the phone."

"British . . . that would have to be Tiffany Prentice, but she's not working today."

And so it goes, she thought. "I know you're not allowed to give out the phone numbers of the staff, but it's very important that I talk to her. . . ."

The nurse was already shaking her head. "Sorry, I can't help you; we don't keep staff phone numbers in the department anymore. Some weirdo got ahold of the list and was making obscene phone calls at all hours of the day and night. You'd have to ask the nursing supervisor or the director of personnel and I doubt very much if they'd make an exception unless it was truly an emergency."

Sydney nodded to show she understood. She could always try the trusty old phone book. "Will she be here tomorrow?"

"No, she has Thursdays and Fridays off."

"I see. Well, thank you." She started to leave and then stopped. "Would you mind if I asked you a question about Miss Prentice?"

"Go ahead."

"Is she involved with anyone?"

The nurse frowned. "Involved. I'm not sure I want to answer that."

"I realize it may seem to be a very personal question, but I've heard rumors that she may have been seeing a doctor, one of the surgeons."

"Really? Well, it happens, I suppose." The nurse set her clipboard down on the counter and used both hands to rub at the small of her back. "I myself have had the inclination once or twice, but never the time or energy. But why do you want to know?"

She showed the nurse her license. "It may be important to a case I'm investigating."

"A divorce?"

Sydney smiled slightly, but didn't answer, content to let her assume whatever she wished.

"Huh. The other woman. I wouldn't have guessed that in a million years."

"Why not?"

"I don't know. Tiffany is such a fastidious little thing ... very tidy and prim and proper. In fact, I can hardly imagine her in bed with anyone, least of all a married doctor. I would think sex a bit too earthy for her—" her expression changed abruptly and she began to laugh, "—unless, of course, she could sterilize the instrument. In more ways than one."

Sydney laughed. "So you wouldn't have any idea who she might be seeing?"

"No. *But* ... there *are* a couple of surgeons with reputations for after-hours procedures, if you know what I mean."

"Can you give me their names?"

"I have to tell you that I'd never agree to testify to any of this in court. ..."

"Don't be concerned about that. In California the majority of divorce actions cite 'irreconcilable differences' as the cause. Proof of one party's infidelity usually goes no farther than the lawyers who arrange the settlement."

"I hope that's the truth," she said, her manner still hesitant, "because I like my job."

"I understand. All I'm looking for is a name, and keep in mind that whatever you tell me will be considered only as a lead, subject to verification."

"All right, then." The nurse glanced around

quickly, as if to make sure that no one was listening, even though they were alone in the room. "Dennis Campbell and Richard Walker."

Although she had been expecting it, she felt a momentary shock at hearing Walker's name. "But to your knowledge neither of them have been linked romantically with Tiffany Prentice?"

"If so, I haven't heard of it. Except . . . now that I think about it, there's been talk that Tiffany may be up for consideration as a circulating nurse on Dr. Walker's surgical team."

Sydney shook her head, not seeing the connection. "Is that significant?"

"You tell me. They'd be working together more often . . . right now she floats most of the time."

"Excuse me? She floats?"

"She works wherever she's needed. She's fairly new on the staff . . . getting chosen for Walker's team would be quite an accomplishment." Her expression soured. "Then again, if it isn't her nursing skills he's rewarding. . . ."

"Is she a good nurse?"

"Very good technically, which is what counts in O.R., although she may be a little too cool for her own good. She lacks empathy, if you ask me. There's a school of thought that suggests that surgery nurses go into surgery because the patient is unconscious and can't make demands on their emotions. I don't know whether I buy that—particularly since I work in surgery myself—but sometimes I'd swear she's made of ice."

Interesting. "You've heard that Dr. Walker's wife is missing?"

"Yes, I—" She stopped speaking, blinked, and then shook her head. "Everyone is talking about that, but I just now realized that whenever the subject comes up, Tiffany pulls a disappearing act of her own."

That could be, Sydney thought, simply a manifestation of her reportedly cold nature, or it could be something more. Guilty knowledge, perhaps?

Don't jump to conclusions, she cautioned herself.

She took a wrong turn and wound up in a hallway that made a sharp left and ended without warning. There were bulky linen carts along all three walls and the effect was claustrophobic.

"Ah, the scenic tour . . ." a loud male voice said from behind her.

She spun to see Victor Griffith eyeing her in amusement, his lanky form blocking her way.

"God, Victor, you almost scared me to death."

One eyebrow quirked. "God Victor . . . I rather like the sound of that."

"What are you doing here?"

"I would think that would be obvious. I'm following you." He pulled up the plastic cover on the nearest laundry cart and peered disdainfully at the folded sheets and towels. "What other reason would I be *here*, of all places? Do you think I would lower myself to searching through someone's dirty linen?"

"Actually, I do."

193

"Hmm. You could hurt my feelings if you're not careful of what you say."

Sydney smiled. "I'll keep that in mind. Why are you following me?"

"You're the detective, figure it out."

"I have other things to do." She started to edge past him, but he moved to cut her off. "Victor . . . get out of my way."

"Answer one question, and I'll step aside."

She gazed heavenward. "Save me from reporters and Englishmen in the noonday sun—"

"I think it's mad dogs and Englishmen."

"Is there a difference?"

Griffith laughed uproariously. "You never cease to amaze me."

"Nor you to annoy me."

"Sydney! I'm crushed." His grin was wicked. "You're welcome to try and manhandle me, if you want me out of your way."

"Ask your question," she said.

"Who did you come here to see? I know it wasn't the eminent surgeon, because *I've* been watching him."

"Why are you watching him?"

"Do you know how vexing it is to respond to a question with a question? But then, I've just done it myself, haven't I? Shit, I can't stop."

"You are insane."

"Even so, I insist you tell me who you came to see."

Sydney considered her options, neither of them entirely satisfactory. The truth would send him scurrying after Tiffany Prentice. On the other hand, a lie might well backfire ... but more to the point, right now she couldn't think of one.

"Come on," he prompted. "Remember who's asking ... I've seldom been fooled."

"All right. I came hoping to talk to a nurse who is rumored to be more than a friend to Richard Walker."

His expression was one of pure delight. "You mean Tiffany?"

She should have known.

"Hell," he said, "why didn't you ask me? Save us both some time."

"Next time I may do that." She regarded him, irritated. "I answered your question, so you answer mine. Why are you following Dr. Walker?"

"Because, my dear—" he smiled archly, "—you drive like a bat out of hell."

Sydney straightened. "That was you? In the van?"

"None other."

"You flaming idiot ... you could have gotten us both killed!"

"*I* could have. *I* could have ... you were the one driving like you were a stunt driver in *Bullitt.*"

"That's it." She feinted to the left and then darted beneath his right arm. Walking backwards down the hall, she glared at him. "Don't you dare follow me, and from now on, stay out of my way."

"Don't you want to know what Tiffany had to say about your client?"

"I'll ask her myself." She turned her back on him and continued walking.

"Well, I'll tell you anyway," he called. "They're in love."

His voice echoed in the hallway.

TWENTY-FOUR

Lights were on in the Dean house when Sydney pulled up out front at a quarter past five, but after she turned off the ignition, she sat in the car for a moment to gather her thoughts.

She was angry still, but at whom?

Victor Griffith had only been the messenger bringing bad news—news that was not totally unexpected.

Walker, on the other hand . . .

If the man could look her straight in the eyes and *lie* that convincingly about his marriage, what else might he have fooled her—and the police—into believing?

Over the years—particularly since she'd become a private investigator—she had met other liars, people who seemingly had a difficult time telling the truth about anything at all. Some actually believed their own lies, however outrageous, and were furious when their honesty was questioned.

A few quite simply didn't give a damn whether anybody believed them or not.

Walker, she suspected, was one of those, supremely confident in his ability to handle any challenge to his version of the truth. To that end, his natural arrogance had served him well.

He undoubtedly was having an affair with Tiffany Prentice, but more than that, according to the surgery nurse, he had a reputation as a man with a roving eye. Which made him a liar *and* a cheat.

Hilary deserved better.

She had to consider the possibility that everything Walker had told her thus far might be untrue. Did he know where Hilary had gone ... where she was right now? He had been alone at the house that evening; he could easily have destroyed whatever evidence his wife had left behind ... or worse.

Sydney realized that sooner or later a confrontation with Walker was inevitable. She could — maybe should — simply withdraw from the case, but she was unwilling to give up on Hilary.

"Damn it," she said.

Complications, she thought, *always complications.*

The door opened, spilling light, and Josiah Alexander stepped outside.

"Miss Bryant."

She thought his tone oddly formal, but then she saw his face more clearly. His mouth was drawn in a deep frown that tugged downward even at the corners of his eyes. "What is it?" she asked.

"The police have been by."

"And?"

He shook his head. "Come see for yourself."

Inside, the house smelled of baking bread and something mildly spicy that she couldn't identify. The front room was immaculate, furnished in Early American style. Hand-braided rugs accented the hardword floor, which was polished to a high gleam.

Lizbeth Dean sat in a chair near a reading lamp. She was leaning forward, her elbows resting on her knees, her hands clasped beneath her chin. She stared without blinking at a point midway across the room.

Tears glistened on the smooth, dark skin of her face. She was a small woman, and the tailored blue skirt and jacket she wore showed her trim figure to advantage. Her hair, streaked with gray, was cut in a modified Afro.

She did not, at first glance, appear to be aware of their presence.

"Hasn't said a word since the police left half an hour ago." Josiah looked completely at a loss. "I don't know what to do for her."

"Were you here when they talked to her?"

"I was." Now his chin jutted defiantly. "They asked me to leave, but there wasn't a chance in hell I'd leave her alone at a time like this."

"What happened? What did they say?"

"Pretty much what you did—that a woman's

disappeared and some witness said that Lionel had made some threats. But they were a little more ... emphatic ... in how they put it. Said the boy's attorney wouldn't be able to plea bargain his way out of *this.*"

"I assume they asked her if she knew where he was. Did she tell them?"

"Can't tell them what she doesn't know," he said, but his manner was not as assured as it had been earlier in the day.

Sydney nodded thoughtfully, and went to sit across from Lizbeth Dean. The old man remained standing, watching them with his worried eyes.

"Mrs. Dean?" Sydney spoke softly, fairly certain that the woman had been listening to what was said, regardless of her lack of expression. "I'd like to help you if I can. My name is Sydney Bryant and I'm a private investigator."

There was not even the slightest response.

"I've been hired to find Hilary Walker—the woman who is missing—and I'll be honest and tell you that I'm the one who gave the police Lionel's name."

Again there was nothing.

"I know he's your son, and I'm sure that you love him, but he may be in serious trouble. Right now it may not seem as though there's anything you can do to help him, but there is."

Her words were followed by a silence that was almost palpable.

To break it, Josiah Alexander cleared his throat and then shifted his weight uneasily from one foot to the other. "Lizbeth?"

Sydney reached to touch the older woman's clasped hands. "I don't know whether or not your son had anything to do with Mrs. Walker's disappearance, but running and hiding won't change the way things are. Eventually the police will find him . . . but it would be better for Lionel if he turned himself in."

A muscle twitched at the corner of her mouth and Lizbeth Dean turned her head slowly until their eyes met. "Better?" she said, her voice husky with tears.

"Yes." Sydney felt a sense of relief and glanced at Josiah who nodded encouragingly. "If he turns himself in and cooperates with the police, this can all be over in a few hours."

"What if he did it? What if he did something to that woman? What if he hurt her somehow? It won't be over then. It won't *ever* be over, then."

There was no arguing that. "If he did, he'll have to be punished—"

"Go to prison, the policeman said."

Sydney did not answer, but she saw she didn't have to.

The woman covered her eyes with her hands and began to rock back and forth. "Oh, Lionel . . . my poor child . . . what's gonna happen to him now?"

With surprising quickness, Josiah knelt by her side and put his arm around her. "Lizbeth," he said, "you know this is the right thing to do. In your heart, you know. You don't want the police

201

hunting him down. . . ."

"But I can't stand to think of my boy in prison." She shuddered. "Locked up that way."

"Try *not* to think of it," Sydney urged. She felt awkward, caught in the middle, trying to comfort a woman whose son still had to be considered a suspect. "Mrs. Dean, no one knows whether Lionel is involved or not. It's too early to find him guilty. All the police want right now is to talk to him."

"Do you really believe that?"

Sydney heard the undertone of skepticism and bitterness in the woman's voice and wondered if there was anything she could say or do that might help.

But Lizbeth Dean wasn't waiting for an answer.

"Lionel's been in trouble with the law for most of his life," she said. "I've done what I can, brought him up the best I could, but every year things have been getting worse and worse. I try to understand what moves him to do those awful things, try to be here for him when he needs me, but sometimes . . . I swear to God . . . sometimes, I don't know him at all."

"Whatever's happened isn't your fault." Josiah patted her on the knee. "The Lord knows you've been a good mother to the boy."

"Maybe it's in his blood to do bad. His papa was no saint, I can attest to that, and they say the acorn doesn't fall far from the tree. Maybe what they say is right, because I tried in every way I know how to make him a good person, and I failed."

"Hush, Lizbeth," he said. "I won't be listening to that kind of talk."

Her mouth twisted into a pale imitation of a smile. "You're a good friend, Josiah, but even you can't deny that I haven't done right by my son." She put up a hand to stop his protest. "Somewhere along the line, I should have asked for help, but I wanted to keep it a family matter. I was too proud to admit that I couldn't handle my own son . . . and too blessed stubborn to give up on him. Even now . . . I can't give up on him."

Sydney lowered her eyes; the look of pure love on the woman's face was almost painful to behold. It wasn't for lack of love that Lionel had gone bad.

"So," Lizbeth Dean said, "I'm going to do the right thing now. I'm going to see to it that Lionel turns himself in."

Sydney glanced up in surprise.

"That a girl," Josiah said, reaching out to pat her hand lovingly.

"Do you know where he is, then?" Sydney asked.

"Yes, I believe I do."

"Mrs. Dean, I would like to talk to him — can you tell me where to find him?"

"It pains me to say it, but it wouldn't be safe for you to just show up suddenly on his doorstep. He knows the police are looking for him. He might do something foolish, and I don't want anyone, *anyone*, to be hurt."

203

Sydney knew she had a point.

Lizbeth Dean was silent for a long moment and then she nodded with apparent satisfaction. "But you come back here first thing tomorrow morning and he'll be here. I'll see that you have a chance to talk to him before we go down to the police station."

TWENTY-FIVE

After making arrangements to return at seven the next morning to question Lionel Dean, Sydney drove to her mother's house to water the plants, as she always did when her mother was away.

She unlocked the kitchen door and went inside. Although her mother had not been gone two full days, the house already had begun to smell stuffy and unlived-in. She propped the door open with a chair, latched the screen, and then walked through the first floor opening windows to let in the fresh night air.

She didn't turn on any lights; the streetlamps provided light enough to see. Even if there hadn't been, she knew the house so well, she would have had no trouble finding her way around.

For now, the darkness suited her.

Back in the kitchen, she stood at the sink and had just begun to fill the watering pot when she saw movement out of the corner of her eye. A dark shape appeared at the screen door.

"Sydney?"

She hadn't been aware of holding her breath, but she released it in a sigh. "Ethan." She opened the screen door and let him in, then latched it again.

"What are you doing in the dark?"

"Watering plants."

There was more than enough light to see his smile. "Ask a silly question. . . ."

"No, really." She went back to the sink and turned off the water. "The plants love it. But what are you doing here?"

"Actually, I'm hiding out. Today was one of *those* days. Nothing went right. I thought I'd get away from everything for a while . . . spend the night at the house and lick my wounds."

"Sounds gruesome."

"It's worse than it sounds."

He followed her into the dining room and leaned against the table as she watered the plants in the windowbox. "You want to talk about it?" she asked.

"Only after I've had a drink."

"Help yourself . . . you know where my mother hides the good stuff."

"That I do. Will you join me?"

She hadn't eaten dinner and a drink might well do her in, but all at once it sounded good. "Sure. Why not?"

Ethan disappeared back into the kitchen. The evidence of his bartending—cupboards opening and closing, the crackling sound made by an old-fashioned metal ice tray, and the tinkle of the glassware—followed her into the living room.

"To today ... for finally being over," Ethan said, lifting his glass.

She touched her glass to his. "Tomorrow."

They stood in the living room and sipped their drinks. There was something, Sydney thought, very comforting about the dark in a familiar place.

"Sydney..."

"Hmm?"

"I talked to Mitch Travis today. He said you and he had worked some things out."

Hearing the guarded tone of his voice, she quickly finished her drink. "He exaggerates," she said. "We talked. Nothing more."

"What *is* it with you and him?"

"There isn't anything." The alcohol, as usual, went straight to her head. A hazy warmth spread through her, and as she moved past Ethan she handed him her glass. She sat on the couch. "Anyway, we're supposed to be talking about your rotten day."

"Travis was part of it."

"Forget Travis."

Ethan put the glasses on the coffee table and sat beside her. "I gave you the same advice, more than once, if I recall."

"It was excellent advice, and I took it. Discussion closed."

"It isn't like you to be evasive. Why won't you tell me what happened?"

"And it isn't like you to hound a witness," she countered. "Besides, it's absurd to be discussing Mitch when you had such a miserable day, and *my* day, if you want to know, was also a bitch."

Ethan laughed. "One drink and you're on your ass. You are the cheapest drunk I know."

"I am not drunk." She was, however, grateful for the cover of dark. She rested her head on the back of the couch. "I just would prefer to hear the gory details of your wretched day."

"All right, I'll tell you, but then *you* are going to reciprocate."

"God, that sounds painful." She was beginning to feel giddy. Strange how one little Black Russian could have such a potent affect.

"First of all, there was a phone call first thing this morning when I got to the office."

She closed her eyes. "That's terrible. No wonder you had a bad day. A phone call."

"Don't rush me. I haven't told you the worst of it . . . it was Jennifer."

Jennifer was Ethan's ex-wife, but he seldom mentioned her. Sydney had never met her. The marriage had begun and then ended while she was living in Los Angeles, but from what she'd heard, it had been a disaster.

"Really? What did she want?"

"Blood, what else?"

"You mean alimony."

"Same difference."

"Well, Ethan, she did give you the best years

208

of her life."

"Eleven months."

Sydney swallowed a laugh. "That ought to be worth something."

"Not what she's asking. Small countries have been run on less."

"I imagine," she said with as much tact as she could manage under the circumstances, "that it must take an awful lot of money to stay gorgeous."

"She isn't gorgeous."

"That's not what your mother told me." She had to rely on hearsay, because Ethan had reportedly destroyed the wedding pictures.

He shook his head. "My mother never saw her in the morning."

"Sour grapes, counselor. You married her, remember? She must have had some redeeming qualities."

"She didn't talk in her sleep."

"Hmm. Don't mention sleep."

"Anyway, she said she needs more money and she wanted to settle it between ourselves rather than involve our lawyers and go back to court."

"That was nice of her."

"Nice! She knows damn good and well that no judge would agree to increase her alimony. She's just trying to use the threat of legal action to coerce me into giving into her demands. That's hardly what I'd call being nice. In fact, the word doesn't apply to Jennifer."

"I remember reading somewhere that Jennifer is the most popular name for little girls; there must be something nice about her name, at least."

"Now there's a frightening thought if ever I've heard one."

"What are you talking about?"

"It scares the hell out of me to think that in millions of homes across the country, mothers are raising armies of little Jennifers."

Sydney smiled. "Don't think about it, then. Anyway, what did you do?"

"What any red-blooded American would do: I told her I'd see her in court. Then I spent half of the morning on the phone with my attorney."

"Damn. The phone again."

He ignored that. "And then a client who told me yesterday, in no uncertain terms, that absolutely, positively, he would never agree to a settlement, changed his mind mere seconds after I'd turned down the opposition's final offer, and then blamed me because I 'should have known' he would wake up this morning and his horoscope would tell him to take the money."

She laughed. "Sometimes you can't win."

"And as if that weren't enough, I've been subpoenaed in a judicial malfeasance case, which means I'll have to postpone my own court calender and spend most of next week in Los Angeles."

"Ugh."

"All right," Ethan said, "now it's your turn."

"I don't know. . . ."

"Come on, now, we had a verbal agreement. Fair is fair. Tell me about Mitch."

The Black Russian made her feel reckless, but she also felt sad. "What can I say, Ethan? He gets to me."

"Even after everything that's happened?"

"Yes. Or maybe because of it."

"I don't understand."

She sighed. "Don't ask me to explain it; I'm not sure I ever could. There's just something about him. All I know is when I see him, when I'm near him, it takes all of the strength I have to keep myself from touching him."

"He's no good for you."

"I know that, but . . . it doesn't stop the feelings."

Ethan was silent for a moment and then he reached to take her hand. When he spoke, his voice was gentle, and she ached at the sound of it.

"Sydney, I only brought it up because I don't want to see you get hurt. When Mitch told me that he'd seen you, all I could think of was how you were then."

She knew he was right. Ethan was the one who'd helped her pick up the pieces when she'd broken off with Mitch. He had taken her to his family's second home in Baja, where Mitch couldn't find her. Away from the rest of the world, she had very quietly healed.

There had even been one night—the night before they returned—when she had seen a look in Ethan's eyes that had made her think that they might finally be ready to admit their strong feelings for each other.

But the moment had passed.

In a way, she'd been relieved; if they *had* started something then, he might have thought she was only on the rebound from Mitch. And she never would have been certain that she wasn't.

"Things have changed," she said. "I told you last night that it's over, and I meant it. I can't avoid seeing Mitch from time to time, but I'm not going to let anything happen between us."

His hand tightened on hers. "The way you say you feel about him, how can you be sure?"

"I'm sure."

She didn't tell him how it was that she knew, but maybe one day. . . .

TWENTY-SIX

It was past midnight when she got back to her apartment. At the door she dropped her keys, and as she bent down to pick them up, she heard the floor creak down the hallway. She slipped her right hand into her shoulder bag and her fingers closed around the .38 Special.

"Hi," a voice whispered.

Nicole Halpern, dressed in a pink robe and fluffy slippers, came up beside her.

"Nicole, you startled me." She withdrew her hand and reached again for the keys. "What are you doing up at this hour? Isn't tomorrow a school day?"

"It is, but I'm not going to school tomorrow."

Sydney noted the determined look in the girl's eyes. "Why not?"

"Miss Delacourt has arranged for one of those color consultants to come to the school and do a *palette* of colors for all of the girls."

"That doesn't sound too dreadful."

"You don't understand. It's a *man*, and we're supposed to wear just our leotards so that he can—as Miss Delacourt says—'drape us in beauty.' I, for one, would rather be boiled in oil."

"I'm sure it won't come to that," Sydney said with a smile as she opened the door. "Do you want to come in for a few minutes and talk? Or would your dad mind?"

Nicole shrugged and followed her inside. "He's not home yet; he had to work late."

"Were you waiting up for him?"

"Actually, I was waiting up for you. I wanted to give you these." Nicole pulled several folded sheets of computer paper out of the pocket of her robe. "I ran the program on the phone numbers on the bills . . . but there was no discernible pattern."

Even though she'd considered the computer search a long shot, Sydney felt a twinge of disappointment. "There was nothing at all?"

"Afraid not. Not by time of call or the day of the week the calls were placed. But I did finally get through to that other number—"

"Great!"

Nicole shook her head. "Not so great . . . it's a pay phone."

"A pay phone." Sydney sat on the arm of the couch. "Why am I not surprised?"

"The guy who answered was a workman on a Cal Trans crew; he said that people kept passing by, ignoring the phone, but the ringing was driving him crazy."

"Did he tell you where the phone booth is located?"

"Yeah. He said it's at a rest stop, just off the I-5 freeway going north. He was out there picking up the trash that people throw out of their cars." She made a face. "That's the kind of a job I'll be qualified for if Miss Delacourt has her way."

Sydney nodded absently, wondering where Hilary Walker would have gotten that number. Why a pay phone, first of all, and then why one in the middle of nowhere?

"I mean, really," Nicole went on, "she doesn't fool me for a second with that fake French accent. If she's French, *I'm* the queen of—"

Footsteps sounded in the hall. Nicole sprang up and ran to the door to look through the peephole.

"My dad," she said, and with a wave she was gone.

Sydney locked the door and then leaned against it, her mind still occupied with finding an explanation that would account for that phone number.

A logical answer eluded her, and she went to sleep thinking about it.

Her dreams were a confusion of images accompanied by a chorus of voices vying for her attention.

"They're in love."

". . . she's never had a lick of sense. . . ."

"Do the right thing...."
"... proper little ladies..."
"Someone had hurt her...."
"... she wasn't afraid of him...."
"... Hilary Walker's blood type...."
"It won't ever be over...."
"... fake French accent..."
"Could you love me?"
"I'll tell you anyway. They're in love."
"They're in love."
"I love my wife."

She woke once during the night, feeling for a moment that the answers were on the verge of becoming clear, and that there was something she must remember. But whatever revelation had brought her out of her sleep vanished with conscious thought.

Her eyes closed and she slept again.

When Sydney pulled up in front of the Dean house at two minutes after seven, Lizbeth Dean and Josiah Alexander were standing outside on the lawn.

"What now?" she said under her breath.

She did not have to wait long for an answer.

"Miss Bryant," Josiah said as she got out of the car, "the police came and took Lionel away."

She glanced from one to the other. "How did they know he was here?"

"We don't know, and the police weren't saying,"

Lizbeth Dean said, "but it might be that one of his *friends* called and told them."

"How long ago was this?"

They exchanged a quick, questioning glance. "Before six is the best I can estimate." Mrs. Dean did not appear to be certain. "They woke me coming through the door. They kicked it open. . . ."

"Which they're gonna hear about at the next city council meeting, I can guarantee that. This isn't Los Angeles, for crying out loud."

Sydney frowned. "I'd better get down to the jail, then."

"We'll be there shortly," Josiah said. "The locksmith is coming to replace the dead bolt, and I've called a friend of mine who's an attorney. . . ."

"I'll see you there." She turned and ran the short distance to her car.

For a Friday, it was relatively quiet at the jail. In the hallway, several well-dressed attorneys from the public defender's office were rehashing the details of a Lakers game.

The smell of disinfectant was strong enough to make her eyes water, but it did nothing to dispel the underlying odor of unwashed bodies.

"Has Lionel Dean been brought in?"

The desk officer did not look up. "You family?"

"No." She pushed the photostat of her license across the counter.

He picked it up and studied it. "No kidding? A private investigator?" He glanced at her with interest. "I'd never have thought it."

Sydney smiled faintly. "Then I must be doing it right."

"Huh. I suppose. But you know, don't you, that you can't see Dean?"

"I know, but I'd like to talk to the arresting officer if I could."

"Well, good luck. The poor devil had to go to court to testify in a felony hit-and-run. You can go on over there, if you want, but it's a zoo on Fridays."

And Mondays through Thursdays, she thought. "Has Mr. Dean spoken to an—"

"Sydney," a familiar voice interrupted, "what a delightful surprise."

She felt a hand on the small of her back, but before she could move, Jake Scott had his arm around her waist, hugging her against him.

"Jake."

"Is there a problem here?" he asked, smiling.

His expression reminded her of a boa constrictor she had once seen at the Zoo moments before it swallowed one of the live mice put in its cage: hungry and loving it. Jake the snake, and, like a snake, he was capable of shedding his skin when the feeling moved him. She also thought him more than a little unscrupulous.

"No problem," she said.

The desk officer pointedly went back to his work, leaving her to the heir apparent of the District Attorney's office.

"Good, good." He drew her aside. "What brings you downtown?"

"Actually, I was looking for you," she lied.

His hand slid up her side to her rib cage. "That's nice to hear, even if it isn't true."

She hadn't expected him to be that perceptive. "Advantage to Scott," she said. "But since you're here, I might as well ask . . . do you know what's happening with Lionel Dean? He was—"

"Yes, I heard they brought him in this morning."

"Is that all you know?"

"Of course not." His glance at her was shrewd. "What's your interest in this?"

"Richard Walker is my client."

"Ah, that's right, I remember now. It must have slipped my mind."

She smiled and shook her head. "I doubt it."

"As you should. But I don't doubt that Dr. Walker would very much like it if someone else occupied our attention for a little while. Is that why he sent you? To see how serious we are about Mr. Dean as a suspect?"

"Dr. Walker didn't send me." She hooked her thumb in the web of Jake's hand and gently pried his hand loose. "He doesn't even know—"

His laugh cut her off. "He most certainly *does* know. And I have to tell you, I've been wondering how much money he'd be willing to pay Mr. Dean to take the fall. Then again, considering the alternative, I'm sure he'd find it a bargain at any cost."

"Come on, Jake. That's absurd, and you know

it."

"I wouldn't be too sure. I mean, what does Mr. Dean have to lose? A few years at most, given the court's predilection towards leniency."

"A few *days* would be intolerable."

"For Dr. Walker, or you or me, yes. But life on the streets isn't that different from prison ... and when he got out, there would be the prize."

"You're talking as though ... as though Hilary Walker is dead."

"We think she is."

Sydney said nothing.

"And we think your client killed her." He thrust his hands in his pockets. "There's just no other answer, Sydney. He's the only one who'll profit from her death. She was heavily insured, but even if she wasn't, the money he would save not having to divorce her—"

"Divorce her?"

He jangled the coins in his pocket. "The paperwork was ready some time ago, apparently. All that remained was to file, and that's when—"

She blinked. "What are you talking about? Ethan would have told me."

"Ethan didn't know. Walker had gone to another attorney for that. Why, I can't say."

"How did you find out?"

"Dumb luck. The second attorney was called out of town on business, and his secretary found the paperwork on his desk. She had another case he'd told her to file while he was gone, so she brought the Walker papers down to the County Clerk's office to take care of both at the

220

same time." He shrugged. "As soon as the case was filed, it became a public record. Mrs. Walker's name had been in the news ... the clerk called and told us."

Sydney could think of nothing to say.

"So ... there you have it." Jake smiled grimly. "Motive and opportunity."

"But you haven't arrested Richard Walker."

"First things first. We prefer to toss the little fish back in before we make the catch of the day. And Mr. Dean may yet be able to tell us something."

"Would it be possible," she asked, "for me to talk to Lionel Dean?"

"Why not? I'll arrange for you to see him as a friend of the court."

TWENTY-SEVEN

Lionel Dean would have been frightening if it weren't for the tears running down his face.

Massively built through the arms and shoulders, he towered over the officer with him. He had a broad forehead and his eyes were hooded and bloodshot. His mouth looked swollen and tender, and his lower lip protruded enough to show pink flesh.

Had he resisted when the police arrested him, and been hit in the mouth for his trouble? She glanced down at his wrists and noticed the handcuffs were on tight. The skin on his knuckles was abraded, and there was dried blood in the creases of his palms.

He stood with his head lowered, shoulders hunched, but even subdued, his was a presence to be wary of.

"Mr. Dean?"

He glanced up quickly, but carefully avoided meeting her eyes. "Yes'm."

"I'd like to ask you a few questions," she said.

"Yes'm."

"About Hilary Walker."

Even with his eyes averted, she saw the sudden fear in them.

"I already told what I know."

Sydney noticed a smile flit across the officer's face, and she frowned. "I'm not with the police. I'm a private investigator—"

He shook his head. "I already told."

"Then let me ask you about Annabelle Swann."

"Annabelle." His mouth worked as though he tasted something foul. "She the cause of this."

"How is that?"

"Wouldn't have no trouble if she acted the way a woman supposed to act."

"I don't understand."

"Taking my kids, like I ain't got nothin' to say about it. Didn't say nothin' ... just took off one day."

"Because you beat her."

"She sassed me. Got a mouth on her. I tried to tell her not to get me riled, but she never would listen."

He spoke without apparent anger, she thought, as if he were a reasonable man subjected to—and victim of—an irrational woman.

"So after she took off, you found her."

"Yes'm."

"How did you do that?"

"Wasn't hard. That new *boy*friend of hers ... I got the license on the fucker's car."

"Hey," the officer said, nudging Dean in the

223

back. "Watch your mouth."

"It's all right," Sydney said, "I've heard the word before."

Dean coughed, then turned his head and wiped his face on the sleeve of his shirt, but not before she saw the faint beginnings of a smile.

"You had the license plate number. . . ."

"Yes'm."

"What did you do then?"

"I got a friend works at the DMV. He give me the address, and I go to see the man."

"And?"

"He moved, but the sister told me where to. That's all there was to it. I went over to the place, and Annabelle was there."

"You kicked down the door."

His eyes turned crafty. "Cops ain't the only ones know how to do *that*."

"I guess not. So you found Annabelle, and when Hilary Walker showed up, you confronted her."

"The lady made a mistake messing with me. I don't care who she is, she ain't got no right to be messing with my family."

"What exactly happened?"

"*She* told *me* to leave, or she'd call the goddamn po-lice." Belatedly, he seemed to remember the officer standing at his side. He licked his swollen lips and ducked his head. "I didn't want no trouble with the lady, but she pushed me, you understand?"

In a strange way, she did. "You did leave, though."

"That time, yeah. My babies were crying, and Annabelle was screaming at me, and I ... I left."

"And when you came back a few days later, what happened?"

"The lady was there again. Filling Annabelle's head with trash about how she was better'n me. How my babies would be better off if she didn't let me come around no more."

His hands, Sydney noticed, were clenched into fists. "What did you do?"

"I don't remember."

Selective memory. "I see. Then let me ask you something else. You were upset because Annabelle had run off with your children—"

"That's the truth," he interrupted. "She ain't got no right to keep my kids from me."

"But you haven't been around ... you haven't been to see Annabelle or your kids in a couple of weeks. Since the day that Mrs. Walker's tires were slashed."

"I been busy." He glowered at the floor.

Sydney regarded him curiously. Was it, she wondered, simply a matter of his having lain low? Being afraid to show his face and stir things up? "Then it's just a coincidence that the last time anyone can remember seeing you in the neighborhood was that day?"

"I ain't responsible for what people remember."

"*Have* you been back to Annabelle's since then?"

"I been by once or twice."

"But you haven't talked to Annabelle?"

He snorted. "I changed my thinking on that. Talking won't change nothing. When the woman comes to her senses, she can find *me*. I can't waste no more time chasing after her, what with her fool ideas." He spoke loftily, as though from a long-held belief.

"Have you seen Hilary Walker since that day?"

"No."

"You're sure of that?"

"Sure as shit. I told you, I ain't seen her. I ought to know who I seen, and it wasn't her."

"But there are a few things that happened which you haven't been able to remember; I want to be sure this isn't one of them." She was careful to keep any hint of accusation out of her tone.

"That lady ... Mrs. Walker? She's not real easy to forget. Didn't back down one whit when I broke the...." His voice trailed off and he frowned.

Sydney, watching him, thought he was telling the truth.

The officer looked pointedly at his watch. "I'm sorry," he said, "but your ten minutes are up."

"Just one more minute?"

The officer considered briefly and then inclined his head in agreement. "One minute."

Lionel Dean had already started to turn, ready to leave. "A minute or an hour, I can't tell you no more, anyway." He lifted his cuffed arms and flexed his hands. "You want to know about the lady, you ask somebody who knows. And that ain't me."

226

"Who does know?"

"Ask her old man."

Sydney blinked. "Richard Walker?"

"Don't know no Richard Walker. The cops been asking me about him, but I never heard tell of him before today. What I mean is, the other one. Ask the other one."

"I don't understand—"

Dean looked exasperated. "You know, the guy she was married to before. Her first old man."

Startled, she said nothing.

"He was there that day. Ask him."

"Minute's up, and this time we gotta go," the officer said, taking Lionel Dean by the arm. They started down the hall.

"His name," Sydney called after them, "did he tell you his name?"

The big man glanced back over his shoulder at her. "I think he said his name's McCullough. Drives a white Camaro."

TWENTY-EIGHT

Why hadn't Walker told her that Hilary had been married before?

Sydney found a phone booth and called his home number. It was nine-thirty, and he had more than likely gone to his office or to the hospital, but she was taking nothing for granted anymore.

"*Buenos dias,* Walker residence." The woman's voice was accented, but very precise.

"Is Dr. Walker home? This is Sydney Bryant."

"No, I'm sorry. He is not here."

"Are you Lupe Martinez?" She had intended to question the maid, but hadn't quite gotten around to it ... now was as good a time as any.

"Yes."

"I would like to talk to you, if I could."

"To me? But why?"

Sydney heard the caution behind the words. "Dr. Walker hired me to look for Mrs. Walker, and I thought you might be able to tell me about when you saw her last. It could be very important."

"If it helps the señora, I will be glad to assist you in any way."

"How long will you be at the house?"

"Oh, I have only started. It will be many hours until I am done."

She wanted to talk to Walker first, to find out if he knew McCullough's full name so that she could start to trace him, but afterwards. . . .

"I'll be there as soon as I can," she said.

The secretary at Walker's office informed her that "the doctor"—as if there were only one—had been called to the hospital for an emergency surgery. When she tried the hospital she was told that he would most probably be in the operating room for several hours.

"Tell him that it is imperative that he not leave the hospital without calling me first," she said, aware that she sounded vaguely threatening. "It is extremely urgent that I talk to him the minute he's free."

"I'll give him the message," the operator said.

She left her answering service number and then contacted the supervisor at her service to stress how important it was that they make every effort to reach her when Richard Walker called.

Last of all, she called Ethan's office. As Walker's attorney—or one of them, anyway—he might have known about Hilary's first husband.

His line rang continually busy, and after three tries she gave up. It would be faster, she thought, to stop by his office on her way to the Walker house.

The ever efficient Miss Valentine Lund peered over the rims of her glasses, which had slid down her angular nose to perch precariously on its tip. She smiled the icy smile of a fanatically professional secretary who sees the unwelcome possibility that her employer's carefully managed schedule might be disrupted.

"Sydney, how nice."

Translated, that was akin to "oh no," but Sydney returned the smile. "Miss Lund. I'd like to speak to Ethan for a few minutes, if I may."

"Oh!" Miss Lund actually winced and then made a clicking sound with her tongue. "He's so terribly busy this morning, and after yesterday . . . are you sure I can't help you?"

"I really need to talk to him."

"If you must." Miss Lunch reached hesitantly for the phone, as though giving Sydney one last chance to come to her senses and cancel her request.

Sydney only smiled and nodded encouragement.

"What on earth are you talking about?"

She sighed. "You didn't know? Walker never mentioned it?"

"No, I didn't know, and he certainly never mentioned anything of the kind. This is the first I've heard of the existence of an ex-husband." Ethan steepled his hands. "Are you sure?"

"Not entirely, no," she said, "but apparently there's a man by the name of McCullough who claims to be Hilary's first husband."

"I distinctly recall Richard's saying that neither of them had been married before. In fact—" he shuffled through a stack of papers on his desk, extracting a single sheet, "—the police report."

Sydney watched in silence as she scanned the report.

"As I thought," he said, glancing up at her, "Richard made no mention of a previous marriage for Hilary when he was asked."

"Maybe he—"

"Forgot?" Ethan finished her thought. "I don't think that's likely."

"Then maybe she never told him."

"The marriage license application specifically requests that information."

"So if she was married before, and she lied. . . ."

"If she lied on the application, the marriage would still be legal, but it would invalidate any contracts made in connection with the marriage . . . such as a premarital agreement."

"Speaking of which . . . I found out this morning that Walker has filed for divorce."

"What? Where did you hear that?"

She outlined what Jake Scott had told her. "I

231

tried to reach Walker, to warn him . . . it won't be long before the word gets out. I'd hate to see him make a statement proclaiming his love and concern for Hilary, and then have Victor . . . some reporter," she amended, "wave the divorce petition in his face."

Ethan nodded, his expression grave. "This situation could get ugly very quickly. I'd better have a talk with Richard."

"When you do, I want to be there. I have a few things I'd like to say to him myself."

As she reached to ring the doorbell, the door silently opened.

"You are here about the señora?" Lupe Martinez smiled, showing the gold caps on her teeth. "I have watched for you. Come in, please."

"Thank you." Sydney followed her into the kitchen. The woman's long black hair was gathered in a ponytail that reached to the middle of her back and swayed as she walked.

"I will work as we talk, if that is all right."

"That's fine." Sydney sat on a kitchen stool. "Miss Martinez—"

"Call me Lupe."

"Lupe. You know that no one has seen Mrs. Walker since last Monday afternoon. . . ."

Lupe made the sign of the cross. "I pray for her."

"Yes." Sydney smiled. "What I wanted to ask was whether you can remember if anything else was unusual Tuesday when you came to the house."

"Unusual?"

The maid's dark eyebrows drew together in a frown. She began to scrub at the top of the stove, which to Sydney's eye already looked spotless.

"For example, was there anything out of place?"

"Here? In the kitchen?"

"In the kitchen, or anywhere else. Perhaps a glass put on the wrong shelf, or a sweater tucked away where it doesn't belong."

Lupe's confusion showed in her expressive eyes. "It is not so easy to remember. On Tuesday I did my work as I always do, but I am not the one to say what is out of place and what is not."

"Did you see Dr. Walker that morning?"

"No. There was no one at home when I arrived. I have a key, and I let myself in."

"How did you find out about what happened?"

"A friend who knows I work for the señorita called me here to tell me. My friend, her name is Consuela, works usually for the Señora Drake, and so she hears many things. At first, I could not believe what she said, but she swore it was true, and later—" she crossed herself again, "—I found it was so."

"What exactly did she tell you?" Sydney found herself suddenly curious about what Mara Drake's maid might have overheard.

"Oh, I am sorry, you ask, what did she say? Only that the señora was missing. Her English is not so good, there is much she doesn't understand, and . . . and she was very upset. Señora Walker very kindly had helped her last year with the immigration papers."

"That was good of her. Do you think you friend would talk to me?"

"You could ask her, if you wish, but she is one to keep her silence with those she does not know. She was tortured many times in her home land. Because of that, she does not trust strangers."

But she had trusted Hilary Walker.

Sydney was silent for a moment, thinking of the next question to ask. The problem was, there were so damned many little pieces that didn't seem to fit, no matter how she looked at them. "Lupe, did you ever hear Mrs. Walker argue with Dr. Walker?"

Lupe's eyes widened. "Oh, no. Never. They were very — how you say? — correct in the way they spoke to each other. Never with raised voices."

"How often did you see them together?"

"Only on special days. Sometimes the señora would have a dinner for a few guests, and I would come to help."

"Did they have guests often?" She was fishing and she knew it.

"Not often. He is busy all the time." Lupe's smile was sad. "At the New Year there *were* guests, and the doctor did not come home from the hospital. The señora made his apologies . . . but after that, there have been no more dinners. No more guests."

"I see." There was nothing much to any of it, she thought, only scenes from a failing marriage. "When did you last see Mrs. Walker?"

Lupe went to the sink to rinse the sponge. "A week ago today. She came home early from her exercise class; she said she was feeling light in the head."

"Was she ill?"

"I do not know. Maybe. The señora was very pale, but she rested for a little while, and later that morning she went out."

Friday had been the day Hilary took the clothing to the Munoz children. And, Sydney recalled, Hilary had told Nina Munoz she'd forgotten something. "Did she take anything with her?"

Lupe turned to her in surprise. "How did you know this? Yes, she had several packages."

"But she also accidentally left something behind?"

"Yes, that is true." The woman's dark eyes showed her amazement. "I found it on the floor in the entryway after she was gone. A small velvet box . . . it fit in the palm of my hand."

"Do you know what was inside?"

Lupe blushed, her face turning a dusky rose color. "I am ashamed to say . . . I opened the box. There were two tiny clips—"

"Clips?"

"Yes, as a child might use in her hair."

"Barrettes?"

"That is right, barrettes. They were made of fine silver, and etched with a design . . . wait, if it is better, I can show you."

"Please."

Lupe smiled and nodded. "Come."

The safe was in the one place Sydney would never have looked: in the dining room floor. Access was through the false bottom of the china cabinet.

The safe was locked, but Lupe deftly dialed the combination and lifted the door.

"Here it is," Lupe said, reaching down into the vault, "right where the señora put it." She handed the box to Sydney.

Sydney took it, but her attention was focused on what remained in the safe. In addition to several good-sized jewelry cases, there was a thick bundle of envelopes, and an expandable pocket file of the type she used to keep canceled checks.

She opened the velvet box and caught her breath; the barrettes were exquisite. The silver shone with the fine patina of age, and a delicate floral design was etched on the ornamental side of the clip.

"It is beautiful?"

"Very." And, she thought, an expensive gift to give to a child. Sydney glanced at Lupe as she put the box on the floor next to where she knelt. "Lupe, I'd like to look through these papers."

"Oh! I don't know . . . these are Señora Walker's private papers . . . I am not sure she would want anyone to see them, even now."

"You won't get in trouble, I promise. If Dr. Walker objects—"

Lupe shook her head. "The doctor does not know they are here. The safe was put in when he was away. She gave to me the numbers because she has trust in me, that I will keep her secret."

"There can't *be* any more secrets, Lupe. There isn't time."

TWENTY-NINE

Sydney gathered the papers from the safe and
went to sit at the dining room table to look
through them.

There were about fifty envelopes altogether, of
assorted shapes and sizes, bound together by a
rubber band. Some were of parchment, others of
onionskin, but the ones she was most interested
in were plain white #10 envelopes, the kind
found in every store.

She separated them—there were seven—from
the rest and fanned them across the table.

All were addressed to Hilary Walker and at
first glance the typeface looked to be the same
on all seven. None bore a return address. The
earliest postmark was August 5 of the previous
year, and the envelope had been mailed from
Santa Cruz, in northern California.

The most recent of the lot was postmarked
February 5, from San Diego . . . a scant three
days before Hilary had disappeared.

Those dated in between August and February — all mailed either on the fifth or sixth of the month — evidenced the progress south of the writer. In order, they had been sent from Monterey in September, Morro Bay in October, Santa Maria in November, Santa Barbara in December, and January's had been posted in Huntington Beach.

Curious, Sydney thought.

She picked up the most recent of the envelopes and pulled out a folded sheet of lined notebook paper. The paper, too, was of a common variety, and would be impossible to trace.

For a moment as she unfolded it, she thought the page was blank, but then she saw the single word neatly printed in the middle of the paper: *know.*

"Know what?" she asked aloud.

She quickly extracted the letters from each of the envelopes and placed the pages in order of the date received. The message read: *I found you. Now he will know.*

Sydney frowned. Who had written the letters? Was Hilary Walker being blackmailed ... and for what? And if the letters were an attempt at coercion, did that have anything to do with her disappearance?

Had she run away, after all?

Sydney leaned back in the chair. The logical assumption was that the letters — if indeed you could call them that — had been written by Hilary's ex-husband, McCullough, first name unknown. Presumably, he had discovered Hilary's whereabouts last August, and had since been slowly making his way to San Diego.

But, even though the letter from San Diego had only recently arrived, McCullough had been in the area long enough to have followed Hilary when she went to see Annabelle Swann a couple of weeks ago.

What else might he have done during that time?

More important, Sydney thought, where was he now? And how could she find him?

Someone passing through town would not put down the roots by which most people can be traced. Passing through, he would not need to change the registration of his car, nor update his driver's license. Neither was there much of a chance that he would vote, buy property, pay taxes, or get married.

All she had to go on was the knowledge that he *was* in town — along with millions of other people — and was driving a white Camaro.

A needle in a haystack?

Sydney shook her head in irritation; there had to be a way to find him.

"McCullough," she said, "what the hell is your first name?"

The answer to that was in a thick brown envelope that she took from the pocket file.

In it, she found a marriage certificate, made out to Hilary Ann Astin and Thomas Clayton McCullough, dated September 11, 1969.

With the marriage certificate were the divorce papers, which included a receipt from the County Clerk, a record of action for dissolution of marriage, a copy of the divorce petition, summons with proof of service, request for default, financial declaration, and both the interlocutory and final decrees.

The legal grounds on which the divorce petition was filed cited irreconcilable differences.

Which could mean anything, Sydney thought.

A notice of entry supplied the book and page number on which the final judgment was entered. The date of final dissolution of the marriage was April 23, 1975.

There was no request for alimony, although Hilary's monthly income back then had been less than six hundred dollars a month. Her occupation was listed as medical registrar, but no place of employment was given. Perhaps because of her financial circumstances, she had acted as her own attorney, *in pro per.*

McCullough, according to the record of action, had worked then as a truck driver.

A truck driver.

Was it possible, Sydney wondered, that Thomas McCullough had been living in the San Diego area for the past seven months? If he still drove a truck for a living, it would be a simple matter for him to mail his little missives from cities along his route.

The postmarks might have been intended to lay a false trail.

What kind of a game was McCullough playing? And what were the stakes?

Lionel Dean was not the only one with a friend who worked at the Department of Motor Vehicles.

A disembodied male voice sternly advised her not to hang up, and promised that her call would be answered "in the order in which it is received." Sydney spent five interminable minutes on hold listening to quasi-classical music, before her call went through.

"DMV, Clairemont office," a familiar – albeit bored – voice said. The characteristic sound of a dot matrix printer was audible in the background.

"Hi, Barbara, it's Sydney."

"Sydney? Is this a small world, or what?" Barbara lowered her voice. "You won't believe this, but I was just about to call you. . . ."

"Is something up?"

"Maybe. Somebody's run a check on you."

That was not what she'd expected to hear. "When was this?"

"A couple of days ago, I think, but don't hold me to that. I only heard about it this morning. My friend over in records saw an article in today's paper about some case you're working on, and he recognized your name. He said he thought it was strange that someone would be investigating an investigator."

"Did he say who requested it?"

"Not in so many words – he was being *very*

cautious, even paranoid—but I gather it was someone with more than a little pull down at City Hall. Are you stepping on toes, Sydney?"

"Not intentionally." She shifted the phone to her other ear. "I guess I'll find out about it if I am. Anyway, the reason I called—"

"You want to run a name."

Sydney laughed. "That obvious, huh?"

"No one ever calls the DMV for fun, so it has to be business. Who's the lucky investigatee?"

Sydney gave her McCullough's full name and his date of birth, which she'd gotten off the divorce papers.

"All right," Barbara said, "I'll get this for you and call you back."

While she was waiting, Sydney returned to the papers. Most of the correspondence related to the death of Hilary's mother early in 1969, settling the details of a rather meager estate. There had been little cash, and no insurance, but Hilary had inherited a small plot of land in the Santa Cruz mountains.

In a separate envelope were the tax receipts on the property, which verified that Hilary still owned the land. Judging by the minimal increase in the assessed value of the three-acre parcel, Sydney guessed that nothing had been built on the site.

Even so, she copied down its location in her notebook.

After an impatient glance at her watch—less

than ten minutes had passed since she'd given Barbara the information on McCullough – she reached for the thickest of the envelopes, and was surprised to find it taped.

Old-fashioned cellophane tape, yellowed with age and cracking, sealed the flap.

Starting at one corner, she pulled at the tape. It came off easily. Underneath the tape, the glue on the envelope flap had long since lost its adhesiveness.

Inside, folded neatly, were several newspaper clippings. They, too, had yellowed; the paper was brittle and the newsprint faded. A faint musty smell came off them.

A second, smaller envelope had been tucked between the clippings.

As Sydney started to open it, the phone rang.

"Write this down," Barbara said. "McCullough, Thomas Clayton. Address as of August 21st is 564 Hill Drive, Fallbrook, California. Male, five foot nine, a hundred and eighty pounds. Brown hair, brown eyes. Class one license, status valid."

"Wait a minute, let me catch up." Sydney wrote as fast as she could, using an original form of shorthand only she could read. "Okay..."

"There isn't much more. No departmental actions, no convictions, no failures to appear, and no accidents. He's clean with us."

"He would be. What about his car registration?"

"Ah, I almost forgot. There's nothing registered in his name."

"You're sure of that?"

"Am I ever wrong?" Barbara laughed. "No, wait . . . don't answer that. Listen, I'd better go."

Sydney thanked her and hung up, then looked with satisfaction at the address in Fallbrook. "I'm on to you now, McCullough," she said.

But as anxious as she was to find him, he would keep, at least for a few more minutes. Her curiosity had been piqued by the newspaper clippings, and she went back to look at them.

The flap of the smaller envelope had apparently come open when she'd dropped it on the table, and she could see a triangular section of a color photograph. With only a part of a face showing – from the eyes up – Sydney knew it was Hilary.

What she hadn't expected was the devastation the full picture revealed.

Bruises discolored the area between her left cheekbone and the corner of her mouth. Her nose appeared swollen at the bridge and was vaguely misshapen, as though it had been broken. Her upper lip had been split.

There were also marks on her neck, the imprints of fingers and thumbs, along with crescent-shaped gouges where someone's fingernails had dug into the vulnerable flesh of her throat.

Hilary looked both younger and older than in more recent photographs. In spite of her battered appearance, her face was achingly beautiful in its youth. Her white blouse – spattered with blood—had been unbuttoned and pulled down around her shoulders to better display her injuries, and still she stood with her head held high.

Yet her eyes betrayed her, for they held no defiance, nor even a glimmer of hope, only the utter misery of someone forever lost.

After a long while, Sydney turned to the next photograph, which showed a close-up of Hilary's throat. Another featured a profile of her face, illustrating clearly the damage to her nose.

Still others showed her naked back with angry red contusions—lash marks?—across her pale skin, and a jagged cut on the palm of her hand.

Gradually it sank in that the photographs were not all of the same beating. In one, Hilary's right eye bulged grotesquely, the skin around it blue and a violent red. Further on, a full body shot showed lash marks from her upper back down to her calves.

The final shot showed a gaping wound about an inch long at the hairline above the right temple. Blood still oozed, and rivulets of it had dried on the side of her face.

There was no expression in Hilary's eyes.

Sickened, Sydney put the pictures back in the envelope. She slipped the envelope into her shoulder bag.

After the photographs, the articles seemed almost tame. They were not, after all, from newspapers, but rather had been cut out of the old "true crime" magazines. Each told of a woman killed by her husband. Without excep-

246

tion, the women had been beaten to death.

In several instances, people had witnessed the attacks, and no one, *no one,* had interfered. One women had lain in her front yard for more than two hours before an ambulance had been called.

The black and white photographs in the magazines were very like those taken of Hilary.

Irreconcilable differences.

THIRTY

The tires squealed as Sydney pulled out of the driveway, turning left onto Nautilus. The Mustang fishtailed for a few seconds before she regained control and accelerated down the hill.

She flexed her hands around the steering wheel, then tightened her grip. Checking the rear-view mirror, she looked into her eyes and saw the anger there.

She couldn't afford to be angry. The heat of emotion would make her reckless, and now was not the time to act on impulse.

Thomas McCullough was, without question, a man capable of violence, a man who would have to be approached with extreme caution.

With effort, she willed herself to calm down.

The rational thing to do was to call the police and let them confort McCullough. As Mitch had said, they had the muscle.

On the other hand, she doubted that what little information she had gathered thus far would be enough to convince the police to go after him. The fact that he had once been married to Hilary Walker did not, of itself, implicate him in her disappearance nearly thirteen years later.

She had no definitive proof that the man had done anything wrong.

Without a sample of McCullough's writing to use as comparison, she couldn't prove that he'd written the letters to Hilary. Nor was there an implicit threat in the message he'd sent.

The photographs only established that, years ago, Hilary had been beaten several times. They did *not* indicate who had administered the beatings.

The articles failed to prove anything, except, perhaps, that Hilary had long been interested in the plight of battered wives.

All Sydney had to go on at this point were her own dark suspicions. If she stated her case strongly, Mitch might agree to send an officer out to talk to McCullough, but that could serve to warn him off.

No, she thought, the element of surprise had to be on her side. As for muscle . . . she had the .38 Special in her shoulder bag.

She had never yet had cause to use the gun — with any luck she never would — but every month she practiced firing it at the shooting range, and she was confident that, if necessary, she would be able to protect herself.

And, as a precautionary measure, she would give Ethan McCullough's address in Fallbrook.

Sydney did not intend to disappear as Hilary had.

She stopped at the Denny's on Torrey Pines Road at La Jolla Shores Drive to use the telephone. The restaurant was crowded, and she glanced at her watch.

Time had gotten away from her ... it was nearly noon.

She put a quarter in the coin slot and punched out Ethan's number. The clatter of dishes vyed with the murmur of voices, and she turned her back on the sounds, covering her free ear with her hand.

"Law office." Miss Lund's intonation conveyed the image of utmost propriety, of black-robed jurists in silent contemplation of justice.

"Is Ethan available?"

"Sydney ... where on earth have you—"

Miss Lund's voice was abruptly replaced by Ethan's: "Where are you? I've been trying to reach you for the past hour."

"Has something happened?"

"Richard is here. I think you'd better come over ... the shit, as they say, has hit the fan."

"What—"

"I'll tell you when you get here," Ethan said, and hung up before she could reply.

It appeared that Thomas McCullough would

250

have to wait.

The office door was locked and Sydney tapped on the frosted glass panel. A second later the door opened half an inch and Miss Lund peered out at her.

"Has he gone?"

Sydney frowned. "Has *who* gone?"

"A thoroughly obnoxious reporter ... apparently he's been following Dr. Walker." Miss Lund opened the door wide enough to let her in, then quickly shut and relocked it. "I told him in no uncertain terms to go away, but he was lurking around out there. . . ."

It had to be Victor Griffith, she thought. "No one's out there now."

"Good. I'd hate to have to use this—" Miss Lund showed her a can of Mace,"—but I will."

"I don't think that'll stop him; if it's who I suspect it is, he inhales that stuff for breakfast," Sydney said. "Is Ethan—"

"They're waiting for you in Ethan's office."

She could feel the tension when she came into the room. Both men were standing, their expressions grim as they faced each other.

Ethan gave a barely perceptible nod to acknowledge her presence, but did not speak. Richard Walker, looking pale, pressed the bridge of his nose between his thumb and forefinger.

She sat down and waited.

Whatever had been said before she arrived was still there between them. By his stance, she could tell that Ethan was exerting tight control over his temper. Knowing Ethan as she did, she knew it would not be wise to test that control.

"Well," Richard Walker said after a minute, "I don't know what to say."

Ethan inclined his head, as if that were what he'd expected to hear. "Try the truth." There was a curious lack of emotion behind his words.

"It isn't that simple."

"Nothing is simple, but you have no other choice. If you want me to try and help you, you're going to have to be honest."

Walker sighed, turning to look out the window. "I've really made a mess of things . . . it's not easy for me to admit even that. I know I shouldn't have lied to you, but at the time I never thought any of this would happen. I certainly never thought the press would be involved."

"But it *has* happened, the press *is* involved, and now we have to deal with that. And you have to understand that there can be no more lies. Because they'll be on you like a pack of wolves if they smell deceit."

"Yes . . . I know." He sighed again, and turned to face them. "I suppose I should begin by saying that I wasn't lying when I said I loved Hilary. . . ."

Sydney winced at his use of past tense.

". . . because I do love her, in a very special way. But in the past few years, I've come to

252

realize that my love for her was not the intense love that a husband feels for a wife."

"How did you happen to come to that 'realization'?" she asked.

"I think you know how, Miss Bryant. I met someone else."

"Tiffany Prentice."

Walker glanced at Ethan before answering. "Yes. But my relationship with Tiffany really has nothing to do with any of this. I didn't mention it because—"

"It absolutely *does* have something to do with this . . . you wanted a divorce," Sydney said.

Ethan held up a hand. "Wait a minute, Sydney. Let him finish."

"I won't attempt to excuse my actions," Walker said. He spoke directly to Ethan this time. "I'm in love with Tiffany, I don't deny that, and I want to marry her. I consulted another attorney about the divorce, not because I wanted to hide anything from anyone, but because I wasn't sure that you would want to be involved, since you know Hilary socially. And I wanted to spare her the embarrassment of that, as well."

Sydney did not believe him. "Why did you instruct the other attorney to delay filing?"

"I hadn't had a chance to discuss it with Hilary." His annoyance showed. "I wasn't about to have her find out when someone served the papers."

"How very considerate. You don't think she knew you were in love with someone else?"

"Sydney." Ethan frowned at her and shook his head. "Go on, Richard."

"To answer your question, Miss Bryant, no. I don't think she knew; Tiffany and I were very discreet. I never wanted to hurt my wife."

Sydney stared into his ice-blue eyes and wondered if he actually believed what he was saying. Self-delusion, in this instance, was very self-serving.

Walker looked away first. "Anyway," he said, "it doesn't matter anymore; I'm not going through with the divorce. And if ... when Hilary comes back ... I'll try my best to make it up to her."

Sydney studied an irregular patch on the ceiling, and waited until Walker had left the room to call the hospital before she spoke. "Do you believe him?"

"This time, yes." Ethan sat on the edge of his desk. "If there are any more lies, he knows that's it—he's on his own. I won't represent him."

"How many attorneys are there in San Diego?"

His eyebrows arched and he smiled slightly. "Which means you don't believe him."

"I don't know. I find it hard to trust someone who has lied to me so glibly before." She got up and walked over to look out the window. "I think Hilary deserves better than this."

"Few of us get what we deserve."

"Hmm. I gather that when you said the shit had hit the fan you were referring to the press taking an interest in the case—"

"I've never seen anything like it; the phone has been ringing off the hook all morning. It seems as though every reporter in town is on this ... you'd think Richard was running for public office."

Sydney smiled at that.

"They know about the divorce petition," Ethan went on, "and somehow they found out about the other woman ... is it Tiffany? They apparently were camped out on her doorstep bright and early this morning ... Richard told me she's gone into seclusion."

"What about the ex-husband, McCullough ... do they know about him yet?"

"Not that I'm aware of, or at least, no one has mentioned that name to me."

"Did you tell Dr. Walker about him?"

"No, but I will as soon as—"

"Tell me what?" Walker stood in the doorway. He had taken off his suit jacket and loosened his tie.

Sydney and Ethan exchanged glances.

Walker came into the room and closed the door behind him. "Is there something I should know?"

"Richard ... the other night, you told the police officer that this was your first marriage. Yours and Hilary's."

"Well, it is."

"But it turns out ... Sydney has come across some information which indicates Hilary had been married to a man named McCullough before she met you."

He blinked twice and then shook his head. "That can't be right."

"I've seen the marriage certificate and the divorce papers," Sydney said. "They were married for about five and a half years."

"Five and a half—" He stopped short and ran his hand through his hair. "She never told me."

Watching him, Sydney saw the change in his eyes. For the first time since she had known him, there was heat in that measured glance.

THIRTY-ONE

Sydney gave Ethan and Richard Walker a capsulized version of what she'd uncovered regarding Thomas Clayton McCullough, and she gave Ethan a piece of paper with the address she had traced him to.

"I was on my way to Fallbrook when I called you." An hour had passed, she noted, suddenly impatient. "With any luck, I'll find him there."

"I hope you know what you're doing," Ethan said. "He sounds like trouble, if you ask me. Are you sure you don't want me to come with you? I can have Valentine cancel my appointments—"

"Don't worry," she said, starting for the door. "If I didn't think I could handle it, I wouldn't go."

Walker, seemingly lost in thought, did not

look up as she passed.

Ethan followed her into the outer office. "Be careful, will you?"

"I always am."

The instant she left the building, she saw the van parked next to her car, and beside it, the lanky form of Victor Griffith.

"What have I done to deserve this?" she asked, *sotto voce*. There was no way to avoid him, and after a momentary hesitation, she started across the parking lot, constructing a story as she went.

Victor spotted her and waved. "Sydney, hello. I was just about to come looking for you."

"Why? I told you I have nothing to say to you."

"Hey, I wanted to show you this." He pointed at the left front tire, which was flat. "Somebody let the air out of your tire."

Sydney counted to ten. "Somebody, huh? Whoever it was is going to wish he hadn't done this."

"Tsk tsk. Revenge is such an uncivilized concept."

She knelt beside the wheel. "If my tire was slashed, it'll be more than a concept."

Victor leaned against the car door, his arms folded across his chest, and gazed down at her. "I know *I'd* be worried if I'd done that. Thank

258

goodness my conscience is clear—"

"I'm sure it is," she said dryly.

"—although I hear that there are some in our fair city who do that kind of thing all of the time and get away with it. And they never give a moment's thought to worrying about retribution."

There was no puncture that she could find. That was a relief, since the tires had cost more than a hundred and eighty dollars a piece.

"Isn't it a shame," Victor continued, "that you'll never *know* who did it?"

"I have a vague idea."

"Really? I must tell you, Sydney, I find it a bit unsettling to think that you would actually associate with someone of that ilk."

She dusted off her hands as she straightened up. "I think you've missed your calling, Victor; you should try for a career on the stage. Or maybe the circus."

His smile widened. "I do believe you're upset about something."

"I do believe you're right." Sydney brushed past him and went to unlock the trunk. "If you plan on staying, you can make yourself useful."

"As much as I'd like to be of assistance, I've got to be off now. Duty calls, and I am but a slave to its every whim."

Looking up, she saw Richard Walker crossing the parking lot. Even from a distance, she could see the angry expression on his face.

Victor half skipped to the van and climbed in. A black puff of smoke belched from the tailpipe as he started the engine, and as he backed out, he narrowly missed hitting her right rear fender.

"Jerk," she said.

He leaned forward and waved to her before taking off after Walker's Jaguar XJ6.

Twenty minutes later, she lifted the flat into the trunk. After wiping the worst of the dirt and grease off her hands, she got into the car and put the key in the ignition.

The car wouldn't start.

At that point she noticed that the hood was ajar. Someone had gotten into the engine compartment. Victor, no doubt.

In the seconds it took to walk to the front of the Mustang and open the hood, the various methods of disabling a car passed through her mind. Some of the more radical possibilities would require a mechanic to set them right.

Luck was with her; he had only disconnected the battery cables.

Even so, another five minutes had passed by the time she pulled out of the parking lot. Traffic was heavy, typical for a Friday afternoon, and she spent ten more minutes getting to the freeway.

At least, she thought, Victor had given up trying to follow her.

The last thing she needed was for him to show up when she located Thomas McCullough.

THIRTY-TWO

Sydney couldn't find Hill Drive on her map, and she had to ask several people before she found someone who could give her directions. It was located, she was informed, on the very outskirts of town.

Hill Drive turned out to be a narrow gravel road that seemed to disappear into a grove of avocado trees. The trees were not well tended, and she could see black, rotting fruit beneath them.

Although it was not yet five, the sky had already begun to darken, the shadows lengthening as the sun neared the western horizon.

She drove slowly, trying to avoid the deepest of the potholes. On either side, the trees rustled in a light wind, sounding almost as though they

262

were whispering.

The road curved to the right and passed through a thick growth of bushes. With a sudden flurry of movement, a covey of small birds took wing, flying directly across her line of sight.

She could not help thinking that this would be a perfect place for someone who wanted to hide. She had seen no one since she'd turned off the paved road, and the natural cover of the orchard would conceal any number of sins from prying eyes.

The road began a gradual rise, but rather than coming clear of the avocado grove, the trees pressed closer, their branches forming a canopy that blocked out the sky. The road curved again, more sharply, and at last a house came into view.

Built of stone and mortar, and set back from the road, it was, in fact, little more than a cabin. The two windows that faced front were shuttered. A carport adjoined the house, and parked beneath its sagging roof was a late-model white Camaro.

Someone, at least, was here.

Sydney turned off the engine and glided to a stop a hundred feet from the house, all the while watching for any sign of the tenant. Nothing moved. The wind had stilled, and the silence was absolute.

Taking the gun from her shoulder bag, she opened the car door as quietly as she could. She started toward the house, fully aware that she would be visible to anyone inside who cared to look out.

A part of her expected to be challenged, to hear a voice to call out and warn her off, but she made it to the front door without incident.

She knocked on the door.

There was no response. Leaning closer, she listened for any sounds of movement from inside, but heard nothing. She knocked again, harder this time, scraping her knuckles on the weather-roughened wood. When there was still no answer, she reached to try the doorknob.

It turned easily in her hand.

Caution prevented her from just walking in. She let the door swing inward until it hit the wall.

The room was dark, with only thin fingers of light showing around the edges of the shuttered windows. Stirred by the draft from the open door, dust motes danced in the air.

After a moment her eyes adjusted to the dimness, and she could make out details.

It would never make *Better Homes and Gardens.*

The main room of the cabin – about nine feet by twelve feet in area – was sparsely furnished, with only a couch, one overstuffed chair, and a wood crate that served as a table. An oil lamp, the glass chimney dark with soot, sat on a corner of the makeshift table among a cluster of generic-brand beer cans.

To the left was the kitchen, equipped with a huge cast-iron stove and an old-fashioned icebox, with a plain wood counter running the short distance between them. There was no sink, only an enamel wash basin, which was full to overflowing with dirty dishes.

An open shelf above the counter held rows of canned goods, primarily soups and a variety of prepared "dinners," including beef stew, spaghetti, ravioli, chili, and corned beef hash.

A plate, apparently forgotten on the stove, was clumped with a half-eaten, unrecognizable meal.

She could smell the spoiled food, a strangely noxious odor that was only partly dissipated by the influx of fresh air.

As far as she could tell, the cabin had no electric lights, no indoor plumbing, nor did she see a telephone. A fireplace, nearly choked with ashes, was the obvious source of heat.

McCullough was certainly roughing it.

Wherever he might be.

There was only one other door, and it was closed. Her first thought was that it led outside, but no light showed from beneath it. A bedroom, then?

"Is anyone home?"

Her voice sounded loud in the cramped space, and even if McCullough was in the bedroom, she was certain he would have heard her. Unless, perhaps, he was asleep.

Or drunk.

She didn't much like the prospect of startling him awake, particularly if he had been drinking, but she wasn't accomplishing anything by delaying the inevitable. She crossed to the bedroom door and hesitated, listening intently for the sound of breathing.

Again there was only silence.

She thought fleetingly of turning back, but she had come this far. . . .

Sydney turned the doorknob with her left hand; her right hand held the gun. The latch bolt clicked as it cleared the striker plate, and, after taking a deep breath, she pushed the door open.

The hinges squeaked, but her first look into the room told her that the man inside would not hear it . . . or any other sound.

He was dead.

She stood motionless, seeing what was before her, but not really taking it in.

The body of a man lay face-up on the floor in the space between the bed and the door. He was barefoot, dressed only in khaki work pants, which were spattered with his own blood.

His blood was, in fact, all over the room.

The walls were speckled with it, and in several places there were thick brownish-red smears of it. As if, she thought, he had braced himself against the wall for support and then, when his legs could no longer hold him, he had slumped down to sit on the floor.

The solitary window, shuttered from the outside like those in the front room, but with several slats missing, showed a fine spray of blood that ran in a diagonal line across the grimy glass.

Blood had saturated the bedsheets, which were tangled in a heap in the middle of the bed.

Worse than all of that was the thick puddle of blood that had pooled beneath the man's battered head. His face had been reduced to pulp, his features resembling nothing remotely human.

One of his eyes had ruptured, and, suffused with blood, it now appeared to be black. The other eye was mercifully closed.

There was a dark stain on his trousers where he had urinated, either in fear during the attack, or after death.

A glint of bone showed in a deep, gaping wound above his left temple.

A darkish, jellylike substance had leaked from both of his ears.

Over it all hung the stench of blood, thick and cloying, the metallic scent of copper.

And the silence. The awful, total silence.

All at once, Sydney began to feel light-headed, and she took a step backwards, out of the room. But even so, the sight of him stayed with her.

"What now?" she whispered.

She hadn't wanted to admit it, even to herself, but she'd almost begun to think that she might find Hilary here, being held prisoner by a vengeful ex-husband. As improbable as that seemed, stranger things had happened.

Thomas Clayton McCullough had made one hell of a good villain.

With McCullough dead—assuming it *was* Mc-Cullough—she had one less lead to follow.

Although ... it was possible that if she searched the cabin she might be able to find something that would tell her what she needed to know. Had McCullough been blackmailing Hilary?

Had Hilary been here?

She knew better than to disturb a crime scene, but she felt compelled to take a quick look around before going to find a phone to call the police.

A couple of minutes would not make a difference to the man in the bedroom.

Her search was actually simplified by the lack of space in the two-room cabin.

There were no closets, no cabinets, and no drawers in which to secret things away. Stone walls did not allow for hidden panels.

A man's leather jacket hung on a nail on the back of the front door. In one of the pockets she discovered an opened pack of unfiltered cigarettes and a cheap disposable lighter. She did not touch either item. The other pockets were empty.

She found a suitcase sitting open on the floor in the hidden recess between the couch and the chair. It was full of soiled shirts, pants, and underwear, all belonging to a male. A superficial examination of the clothing revealed nothing of interest.

She did not come across whatever blunt instrument had been used in the attack, but she did find a few small drops of blood in the approximate center of the main room. She was careful to step around them.

Nowhere in the cabin did she find even a scrap of paper that might help identify the dead man. If he had a wallet, it was probably still on the body, which she did not dare to disturb.

The only other place to look was the car.

She glanced at her watch, feeling pressed for time, and then went out to look through the Camaro.

The car wasn't locked, but it took several minutes to get the door opened without disturbing—or leaving—any fingerprints. The interior smelled of stale cigarette smoke and a more pungent odor she recognized after a minute as brake fluid.

Inside she reached across to open the glove compartment, hoping to take a look at the registration, but it was locked, and she had no keys.

And no time to jimmy it.

Under the driver's seat she found a crumpled receipt for twelve gallons of gas and a quart of oil from a Chevron station in Oceanside. The charge slip was stamped with Thomas McCullough's name and was dated February 10, two days ago.

The scrawled signature was all but unreadable.

In the back seat of the Camaro she found several plain white #10 envelopes, similar to those sent to Hilary. Using the barrel of the .38, she flipped them over, but none bore an address.

And that was it.

She put the charge slip back where she'd found it and got out of the car.

It was time to call the police.

THIRTY-THREE

Fallbrook was within the jurisdiction of the San Diego County Sheriff's Department. Unsure of which was the nearest sheriff's station, she called the Communications Center to report the discovery of a dead body.

A second quick call to Ethan, and then she returned to Hill Drive. It was fully dark now, and her headlights did little to dispel the shadows.

She parked near where she had parked before, and waited for the silence to be broken by the wail of sirens that would signal the arrival of what she'd always thought of as "the cavalry."

At first only a single patrol car responded, but before long, others had followed – murder scenes could always be counted on to draw a good crowd – and within minutes the narrow road was nearly blocked with police vehicles, all with their emergency lights flashing.

The first deputy took charge and immediately

cordoned off the crime scene, stationing men along the perimeter to keep anyone—including other policemen—from destroying the evidence.

As she'd known he would, the deputy insisted that she not leave until someone had an opportunity to question her. To keep out of the way, she sat alone in her car, and from there she watched.

The lab van showed up a little before six-thirty, and the evidence technicians hurried into the cabin. A few minutes later, they set up the generator-powered floodlights to light the scene.

No one had come yet to remove the body.

The body . . . .

Only once before had she been involved in a murder case.

It had happened in Los Angeles, where she'd gotten her training as an investigator. The victim had been a fifteen-year-old runaway, who had turned to prostitution to keep from starving.

"You'll be chasing smoke," her boss had warned her. "Those kids are phantoms . . . they seem to vanish in the light of day."

But Sydney had kept at it, working every angle she could think of, and had managed to trace the girl from Hollywood to Malibu to Venice Beach, but in the end, she'd been too late to save her.

The young girl's "fancy man" had taken her out to a deserted canyon, put a collar around her neck and attached a leash, then made her run after his car to teach her to be "a good dog." When she could run no more, she had fallen. Her neck was broken.

The blood and tracks in the dirt showed that her body had been dragged for more than a mile.

Sydney had accompanied the parents to the morgue to make the identification.

After that, she'd had nightmares for several weeks, and even now she could remember that young face. Part of it was guilt. She could not help but wonder whether, if she had worked harder, or had asked the right question of the right person a day earlier, the girl would be alive now.

She would never know.

Determinedly, Sydney made an effort to think about something else.

Ethan.

When she'd called to tell him about finding McCullough dead, Ethan had wanted to drive out to be with her, but she had pointed out that there was no guarantee that he would be allowed in. The cops undoubtedly would have closed off the road to keep out the curious.

Reluctantly, he'd agreed, and they'd arranged to meet at his office after the police had questioned her.

"Be careful of what you say about Hilary Walker," he'd cautioned. "We don't know that this has anything to do with her."

"What else could it be?"

"A coincidence. From what you've told me, McCullough apparently has been hanging out with a rough crowd."

"I don't know—"

"Or it could have been just about anything. A drug deal that went sour, or maybe it was a random killing and he was simply unlucky enough to have been in the wrong place at the wrong time."

She hadn't argued—there wasn't time—but she'd never had much faith in coincidence.

What, after all, were the odds on a man's being murdered five days after his former wife mysteriously disappeared? A million to one?

In her heart Sydney knew that coincidence had nothing to do with it.

Somehow, in some way, everything that had happened thus far was connected.

And Hilary was the key.

It was after eight before anyone had time to question her.

The homicide investigator glanced at the card she'd given to the first deputy and then looked at her skeptically. "You're the P.I.?"

Sydney nodded.

"You discovered the body?"

"Yes."

"You mind telling me what were you doing way out here in the middle of nowhere?"

"I was looking for Thomas McCullough in connection with a missing persons case I'm working on."

"Well, you found him." He put her business card in his shirt pocket and hooked his thumbs in his belt. "Not that he'll be answering any questions."

"It is McCullough, then?"

"Oh, yeah, it's him. Mr. McCullough has made his presence known around here. That's him, all right. The poor bastard."

Sydney frowned. "Exactly how did he make his presence known?"

"I believe *I'm* the one who's supposed to be asking the questions, Miss Bryant," he said mildly. "But I'll tell you this much ... I can't think of anyone hereabouts who'll lose any sleep over the fact that he's dead." He nodded for emphasis. "Anyway, that's neither here nor there. So why don't you just tell me what happened here tonight? Starting from the beginning."

"There's not much to tell. As I said, I came to talk to Mr. McCullough. I knocked, but nobody answered. The front door was unlocked so I went inside—"

"Are you in the habit of entering houses without permission?"

"Not in the habit, no."

"Good thing. You could get into a lot of trouble that way. If Mr. McCullough hadn't been indisposed, he might not have taken kindly to your inviting yourself in."

"I suppose not."

"On the other hand, I have to admit I'm glad you came across him before he got ripe, if you know what I mean. It smells bad enough in there as it is. Now, go on with what you were saying."

"Once inside I called out ... but there was no answer. Since his car was here, I thought maybe he was asleep and hadn't heard me, so I went to the bedroom, and ... you know what I found."

"He was dead when you got here?"

"Yes."

"What did you do then? Did you touch him or anything to make sure he was dead?"

"No, I didn't touch him. But I could tell by looking at him ... he wasn't wearing a shirt, and postmortem lividity had begun to set in."

The homicide investigator raised his eyebrows. "I guess I shouldn't be surprised that you'd know about that, although it used to be that only the cops and medical examiners were aware of such gruesome details. So much for professional secrets. ..."

"At any rate, I saw he was dead, and I called it in."

"That's it?"

She hesitated and then nodded. "That's it."

"You saw no one other than McCullough?"

"No."

"No one passed you on the road?"

"No."

"What time did you get here?"

"Around five."

"And your call was logged at five-fifty-seven. It took you fifty-seven minutes to find his body and drive back to a phone to call in?"

She'd been expecting that question. "After I'd seen ... what was in the bedroom ... I needed some time to get myself together. I sat in my car for a few minutes, or at least I thought it was only a few minutes."

"Hmm."

His skeptical look was back, but he did not challenge her.

"Is there something else you want to ask me, or can I go?"

For a moment he only stared at her, but then he nodded. "I guess that'll do it, Miss Bryant. You'll need to come in to the station and sign a statement, and we have to take your fingerprints for comparison with any we find inside, but it can wait until tomorrow."

"Thank you." She turned to walk back to her car, but stopped in the middle of the road. "Excuse me, but now may I ask a question?"

He shrugged. "Go ahead."

"Earlier, when you said he'd made himself known ... what was it he did?"

"Nothing illegal, or we'd have run him in so fast his head would *still* be spinning, dead or not. But Thomas McCullough was a mean-looking, crude-talking, scary son of a bitch, and we were always getting calls from women complaining that he was mouthing off ... making lewd remarks, suggestive comments, that sort of thing."

277

"I see."

"And it wasn't just the ladies who wanted to be rid of him; he was the kind of a man who made everyone a little nervous. The kind of a man who when you look in his eyes you just know he's capable of anything. I thought he was crazy, myself."

"So what did you do?"

"Nothing much we *could* do about it, except let him know we were keeping an eye on him . . . it's not against the law to be a slimy bastard, though I'd venture to say, it may have gotten him killed."

They both looked toward the cabin where the body was finally being taken out on a stretcher.

THIRTY-FOUR

When she reached the end of Hill Drive and was waiting to be passed through the road block, she saw the cluster of reporters who had gathered across the road, and swore under her breath.

There, towering over the rest of them, was Victor Griffith. He was gesturing wildly as he talked to one of the deputies, and something about the expression on his face was unsettling.

Of course he would be here; he was a reporter, and murder, even in these violent times, was still news. His van was no doubt equipped with a radio scanner with which he could monitor the police calls.

But he didn't appear to be getting information; he seemed to be *giving* it. At least half of a newsman's job was to listen, and yet she had not seen the deputy open his mouth once.

As soon as the way was clear, she pulled across the paved road, stopped on the shoulder, and rolled down the passenger window.

They were still too far away to hear the conversation, but whatever Victor was saying had the full attention of the deputy, who after a minute raised his walkie-talkie and spoke into it.

Victor smiled with satisfaction.

Sydney thought about that smile all of the way back to Ethan's office in La Jolla.

Given the late hour, it was not surprising that the building was deserted when she arrived. Ethan had given her a key to the outer lobby doors, and she went inside, then locked them after her.

Once the traffic noise had been closed out, the only sound was the hum of the elevator on its way down.

"I saw you drive up," Ethan said when the elevator doors whooshed open. "I was beginning to worry. Are you all right?"

She smiled wearily. "I'll let you know."

"Poor kid . . . even as a cop I never got used to the dead bodies." He drew her into the elevator with him and pushed the button for the third floor. When they started up, he turned to her. "You look tired, Sydney. Are you sure you want to talk about it?"

"It's either talk about it now or think about it all night."

"Some choice. But ... I made a few calls, talked to a few people, trying to get a line on this thing. Then we can brainstorm, see what we come up with."

"I'm going to need all the help I can get."

"It's that bad?"

She frowned. "It's just so damn frustrating. I thought I was getting close to an answer. When I dug up McCullough, I thought I was finally onto something. Now I don't know. I feel as if I'm being led through a maze, and there's no way out."

The elevator stopped and they walked the short distance through the darkened corridor to his office. Ethan held the door for her.

"You've had tough cases before."

"Yes, but never with so many loose ends," she said as she followed him into the inner office.

"Still, you've made progress."

"I'm not sure I'd call it that. I haven't found Hilary. I'm not sure I'm even on the right track. What if I've wasted the past five days?"

Ethan's expression was grim. "Maybe ... maybe Hilary can't be found. Not by anyone."

"You think she's dead."

"I think she's *gone*. Dead or alive, I don't believe that anyone will ever find her. There are two hundred and forty million people in this country—it's not that difficult for one person to disappear, intentionally or not."

Sydney studied him intently. "But why? And *how?*" From the beginning, the odd circumstances of Hilary Walker's disappearance had

281

bothered her.

"I don't know that we can ever hope to understand why anyone does anything," Ethan said. "Why didn't Hilary tell Richard she'd been married before?"

"She might have been ashamed. She'd been horribly abused and yet she stayed with McCullough for five and a half years. Maybe all she wanted to do was forget, to put the past behind her."

"Then why do volunteer work with battered wives? Don't you see? There's no consistency to her actions—"

"Except," she interrupted, "Hilary cared. Her actions may have been contradictory, but her feelings never were. I think more than anything else in her life she wanted desperately to help those women, because she'd been through it herself."

"And now the man who allegedly abused her turns up murdered."

She saw the speculative look in Ethan's eyes. "You've changed your mind about all of this being a coincidence?"

"Now that I've had a chance to think about it, there are a few possibilities that come to mind—"

The phone rang and he reached to answer it.

Sydney moved to the window, and stared out at the night. The possibilities. Including that Hilary could be a suspect in McCullough's death.

Turnabout is fair play.

Earlier today she'd considered it a possibility that McCullough had been after Hilary, despite the fact that thirteen years had gone by since their divorce.

She had thought it possible that it had taken him that long to find his ex-wife.

It had been easy to imagine McCullough the instigator and Hilary the victim. He the villain and she is innocent prey.

What if it was the other way around?

Perhaps having McCullough suddenly reappear in her life had been a kind of an emotional catalyst for Hilary?

"Sydney . . ."

Something in Ethan's voice made her turn quickly.

"Pick up the other phone." He pointed to a wall phone near the bookcase. "I think you'd better hear this for yourself."

She nodded and crossed the room.

"Go ahead, Mike," Ethan said when she was on the line. "Repeat what you told me."

"What I said was, they've already got a suspect on the Fallbrook thing. The name is Richard Walker, and—"

"Walker?" Sydney glanced at Ethan who merely shook his head.

"—and they're trying to locate a judge to sign the warrant for his arrest. I guess Friday night's not the best time to find a judge, or they'd be knocking on this Walker's door."

"What've they got on him, do you know?"

"From what I've hear, they apparently have a

witness who followed him to the scene not more than an hour before the body was found."

Griffith, Sydney thought. It has to be.

"Anyway," Mike continued, "Walker was seen coming and going, and he spent enough time inside to have killed the guy."

"Is that all?"

"They're still working on the physical evidence at the scene, but they figure they've got probable cause, and they want to pick Walker up before he has a chance to destroy whatever evidence he might have carried away. You know the drill."

"Damn." Ethan ran a hand through his hair. "Well, thanks for the information, Mike. I owe you one."

"You owe me at least three, but who's counting? Listen, I gotta go."

Sydney hung up as they did. Ethan seemed preoccupied with his thoughts, and he didn't look up as she came up to the desk.

"Why would Walker go to see Thomas McCullough?" she asked.

He shook his head. "That's what I'd like to know. I can't believe he'd do something so damned foolish, although he *was* pretty upset when he left this afternoon." Ethan reached for the phone and started to dial.

She remembered the anger she'd seen in Walker's ice-blue eyes. And, just as clearly, she remembered Thomas McCullough, lying dead on the floor.

"Damn, his line's busy. I'd better get over

there before the cops show up. Want to come along?"

"I wouldn't miss it."

She followed Ethan to the house and pulled in behind the red Mercedes. A Honda Prelude was parked alongside Walker's Jaguar.

Sydney could hear music coming from the house. Soft, romantic, it was not at all what she thought would be to Richard Walker's taste.

Then, quiet but unmistakable, she heard the sound of a woman's laughter.

THIRTY-FIVE

"Ethan," Richard Walker said, and laughed uneasily, "this *is* a surprise. What—"

"Something's come up and it can't wait. May we come in?"

Walker hesitated for only a second. "Of course."

He stood aside and nodded a greeting as Sydney passed by him. She noticed that sliding doors had been drawn across the entry into the dining room. The music had been turned off.

The faint scent of perfume lingered.

When they were seated in the living room, Ethan leaned forward, looking intently at his friend. "I have to ask you a question, Richard, and I want a straight answer."

Walker glanced from Ethan to Sydney and back again. "Go ahead."

"Why did you go to see Thomas McCullough?"

"How on earth did you find out about that?"

"Never mind how, just answer the question."

286

Watching Walker, Sydney saw a flicker of annoyance cross his face; he wasn't used to being treated this way, and he obviously didn't like it.

"Well, actually, I thought he might know where Hilary is, given their former . . . relationship. I decided to ask him. It was that simple."

"You hired me to find your wife . . . why not leave Mr. McCullough to me?" Sydney had agreed to let Ethan do the talking, but it bothered her that Walker seemed to be disregarding her efforts.

Walker lifted his shoulders in an elegant shrug. "To be honest, Miss Bryant, I wanted to see the man for myself. All of this—the news of Hilary's previous marriage—had come as quite a shock, and I was curious. I saw no harm in asking a few questions of my own."

"How did you know where to find him?" Ethan asked.

"When you left the room for a moment, I looked on your desk and found the address Miss Bryant had given you. And I went out to talk to the man. It turned out to be a waste of time, but—"

"*Did* you talk to him?"

"I . . . no, not really."

"Why not?"

"He was drunk." The corners of Walker's mouth turned down in disapproval. "Blind, stinking drunk—"

"Dr. Walker," Sydney interrupted, "what time did you get to McCullough's place?"

"A quarter to four, as near as I can recall.

Perhaps a few minutes later."

"How long were you there?"

"Not long at all. Maybe five or ten minutes. As drunk as he was, I figured McCullough was incapable of answering my questions, even if he was inclined to do so. Which I doubted."

"He was alone?"

Walker nodded. "Little wonder at that; the place was a pigsty."

"Was the bedroom door opened or closed?"

"I wasn't aware there *was* a bedroom. McCullough was lying on the couch when I arrived, and I assumed that he slept there."

Sydney exchanged a glance with Ethan. "When you left, he was still on the couch?"

"Wallowing in squalor, yes."

"And you saw no one else?"

"I wasn't looking," Walker said. His eyebrows drew together in a frown. "What is this? Why all these questions about McCullough?"

Ethan cleared his throat. "You don't know?"

"No, I don't."

"McCullough's dead, murdered," Ethan said, matter-of-factly. "Sydney found his body about an hour after you left. The police know you were out there, they've got a witness who saw you, coming and going. You're the prime suspect, Richard."

The muscles in Walker's jaw clenched. "What in the hell are you talking about? Why would I be a suspect? I don't even know the man."

"The 'why' has little to do with it. They don't have to prove motive. The fact is, they're obtain-

288

ing a warrant for your arrest."

"That's absurd!"

"Try telling them that."

"I'll deny I was ever there. They can't prove otherwise."

"Don't be a fool," Ethan said. "Don't forget they have a witness, and—"

"So it'll be my word against his. Who are they going to believe?"

"Dr. Walker," Sydney said, "the witness who saw you is the reporter you sent me to talk to. Victor Griffith. He's been following you for a couple of days now, and he always carries a camera. He may have photographs of you going into McCullough's cabin."

He narrowed his eyes, but said nothing.

"And," Ethan added, "there'll be physical evidence. One of the principles of crime scene investigation is that every time a person goes into a given room, they take something away and leave something behind. It might be microscopic—fibers or dust—but it's there. And if it's there, they'll find it."

Walker remained silent.

"It'll do no good to deny what they can prove." Ethan glanced at his watch. "They'll be here soon, Richard. We'd better go over the rest of what happened while we have the chance."

If he heard, Walker gave no sign of it. He stared without expression at the floor.

From the direction of the dining room came a muffled, scraping sound. The sliding door? Sydney looked at Ethan, who shook his head.

Enough, his eyes warned.

But thinking about someone's listening silently from another room raised a question in her mind. Could the killer have been waiting in the bedroom at the cabin while Walker was there?

If so, McCullough had to have known of the other person's presence; given the small confines of the cabin, there was no way anyone could have gotten past him without being seen.

Which meant, she thought, that McCullough may have been an accomplice in his own death by helping the killer hide from Walker.

And who would have felt the need to hide from Walker?

"Dr. Walker," she said, "did McCullough know who you were?"

Walker frowned, then nodded slowly. "I'm not sure, but yes, I think he did."

"What did he do to give you that impression?"

"I don't know. As I said, he was drunk, and . . . incoherent."

"He didn't say anything at all while you were there?"

"I suppose he must have—he was raving off and on—but I can't remember anything specific that he said."

"Try to remember," she urged. "It might be important."

"But I don't. . . ."

She decided to try another approach. "Did you say anything to him?"

"Well, I asked if he was Thomas McCullough."

Walker rubbed at his chin thoughtfully. "He didn't answer directly, but he . . . he laughed and said, 'What of it?' "

"Go on."

"As I told you before, he was too drunk for rational conversation, but–" his brow furrowed in concentration, "–he did say something like, 'Don't waste your breath, I got nothing to tell you.' "

"Anything else?"

Walker shook his head. "Nothing repeatable. He became quite abusive . . . started swearing a blue streak."

"When you say abusive, did he threaten you?"

"I suppose it depends on whether or not I was the 'fucker' he was referring to. But he couldn't even stand up. He was very literally falling-down drunk."

Ethan, who'd been listening without comment, got up and went to the door. "The police are here," he said.

THIRTY-SIX

There were three patrol cars, two from the County Sheriff's Department, and one from the city police. They were keeping a low profile—no flashing lights—presumably in deference to the wealth of their surroundings.

Mitch Travis was with them.

Sydney caught his eye, trying to gauge whether he felt the arrest was a right one. His wink suggested that he did.

Standing beside her, Ethan had become suddenly tense.

The first of the deputies walked up to where they waited on the doorstep. "Dr. Richard Walker?"

Walker nodded.

"Dr. Walker, I have a warrant for your arrest."

Ethan took a step forward. "What's the charge?"

"Suspicion of murder."

"May I see the warrant?" Ethan asked, holding out his hand for it.

The deputy's irritation was evident. "And who might you be?"

"It's all right," Mitch said. "He's Walker's attorney." He smiled agreeably at Ethan, who did not return his glance.

The deputy handed the warrant to Ethan. "The warrant further grants us the authority to search the premises for clothing which may have been worn in the commission of the murder of Thomas Clayton McCullough, and to search or impound a 1988 Jaguar XJ6 which was observed at the scene."

Ethan stepped back under the porch light, his attention focused, for the moment, on the legalities.

"Dr. Walker, if you would, please." The second deputy had come up, and he pulled a set of handcuffs from his Sam Browne belt.

Walker held out his wrists.

"You have the right to remain silent," the deputy began. "If you give up that right, anything you say can and will be used against you in a court of law. . . ."

Ethan looked up. "He has nothing to say."

The deputy shrugged. "We didn't think he would." He escorted Walker to the first patrol

293

car and helped him into the back seat.

"All right," the first deputy said, "I'll check inside, and Simmons, you look through the Jag."

"Wait a minute," Ethan said. "I'd like to be with you, if you don't mind, when you go through the house."

"If you're worried we're going to exceed the authority of the search warrant, don't be. There isn't going to be a 'fruit of the poisoned tree' in this case."

"Then you won't mind my tagging along."

"No problem, counselor."

They went inside, leaving Sydney alone with Mitch Travis.

"So . . . you got him. For now."

Mitch shrugged. "*I* haven't got him. I'm only an observer."

"Why is that? I thought you were hot on his trail."

"Let's just say the trail turned out to be a detour, and leave it at that."

"Come on, Mitch. What's going on?"

"You don't really expect me to answer that, do you?"

"Why not? Just between us."

"Between us? I wonder. I think if I told you, you might find it a difficult secret to keep. And Ethan's on the other side in this one."

Something in his eyes made her wary, but she pressed on, determined. "I won't tell Ethan."

Mitch smiled. "You know, I may just tell you,

if only to enjoy the prospect of you leaving him out in the cold for once." His eyes flicked past her toward the open door, and he took her arm, guiding her off the porch to where they wouldn't be overheard. "I mean it, though, kid. If I tell you and it gets back to Ethan, I'll see what I can do to get your license pulled."

Sydney knew it wasn't an empty threat, but the prospect that the case had been broken was too tantalizing to ignore. "You have my word," she said.

"As long as you understand the game rules." At her nod, he continued: "The reason I'm out of it is that we now know that Walker didn't harm Hilary on Monday, because she was alive and well yesterday."

"How do you know that?"

"She was seen at McCullough's cabin. We have a positive identification."

Sydney felt a mixture of relief and confusion. "Who saw her?"

"One of McCullough's neighbors is an amateur artist. She was out sketching, and she saw Hilary walking along Hill Drive toward the cabin. She thought it was odd to see a woman on foot out there, and when she heard McCullough had been killed, she called the sheriff's office. She'd made a sketch of Hilary, and then she identified a photograph. It was definitely Hilary she knew. And since then, they've been able to match Hilary's fingerprints with some they lifted at the cabin."

"What time was this? When she was seen?"

"Near sundown."

It gave her the strangest feeling to know that she had come within twenty-four hours of finding Hilary. Her feelings must have shown on her face.

"You were a step or two behind her, Sydney. You did a good job. You might even have found her if. . . ."

She glanced at him. "If what?"

"If things were different." He sighed. "We think she's dead."

"No—"

"We think Walker killed them both."

She could think of nothing to say.

"There were two types of blood in the cabin," Mitch continued. "The lab boys worked their asses off typing the samples. Most of it was McCullough's, but there was enough of her blood type to raise the possibility that she may have been killed there, too."

For a second she closed her eyes. Had Hilary died in that wretched place? It couldn't be. "Have you . . . where's her body?"

"We haven't found it yet."

"But that doesn't make sense. If Walker killed her there, her body should still be there. It couldn't just disappear. . . ." *As she had.*

"I said, we don't know."

"But you have a witness," she insisted. "He

296

saw Walker go to the cabin. How could he have missed him carrying a body out?"

"Our witness had parked a distance up the main road, so Walker wouldn't know he was being followed. The witness had to walk in *and* out. He got to the cabin several minutes after the good doctor, and lost him altogether when Walker left."

"You think Walker murdered two people and loaded Hilary into the trunk in the space of a couple of minutes?" She did not try to keep the incredulity out of her voice.

"Five minutes is all he'd need. Knock out McCullough, take care of Hilary, put her in the car, then go back in and finish the job."

"Take care of Hilary." Sydney rubbed her bare arms to warm them; it seemed as though her blood had gone cold.

"It's pretty desolate up there. He could have dumped the body anywhere."

"But why would he do it? Why kill her now? And why McCullough?"

"You know why. Better than I do."

Sydney said nothing. Could it be that she had come so close to finding Hilary, only to fail? Worse, if Mitch was right, had she led Walker to his wife?

"Lieutenant . . ."

They both turned in the direction of Simmons, who stood near the opened trunk of the Jag. "Take a look at this, will you?"

Mitch did not hesitate. Sydney followed.

The flashlight shone into the recesses of the trunk, but at first she did not see it. Then she noticed a dark, irregular-shaped spot near the fender wall.

"Blood," the deputy said.

THIRTY-SEVEN

The deputy who had searched the house brought out several items in evidence bags, but wasn't saying what he'd found. Judging from the look on Ethan's face, whatever it was, Sydney knew it wasn't good.

For the second time in three days, Sydney watched as the police took Richard Walker away. She waited until the taillights of the cars vanished around the bend in the driveway, then started in the direction of the Mustang.

The front door of the house opened, and a British-accented voice called after her.

"Where are they taking him?"

In the excitement, she had all but forgotten about Walker's female guest. *Tiffany*, she thought, turning to face her.

The woman standing in the lighted doorway was devastatingly beautiful.

Walker's fortune cookie.

Tiffany Prentice, despite her accent, was clearly of Chinese descent. Her straight black hair cascaded over her slender shoulders, reaching to her waist. Her skin glowed like burnished gold. She was dressed in a silk dress with a mandarin collar, blood-red in color.

"You are the private detective?"

Sydney nodded. "Yes. Miss Prentice, isn't it?"

"Tiffany. I do prefer to be called Tiffany."

It was fascinating, in a way, to hear the British intonations spoken by such an exotic creature. "Tiffany, then. To answer your first question, they've arrested Dr. Walker."

"That is unfortunate." Not a hint of emotion showed on her face. "You know about my relationship with Richard?"

"Yes."

"Then you know he's told me everything." Tiffany drew the front door closed behind her and stepped down off the porch. "You may not believe me, but I am sorry about all of this, what has happened. And I'm sorry for Hilary. She was very nice."

"You've met her?"

"Yes, once."

Sydney regarded her coolly. "Would you mind if I ask what Dr. Walker's told you?"

"That Hilary had found out. About us."

The man was a consummate liar; only this afternoon he had denied vehemently that his wife was aware of his deceit. Her head ached from all of the lies.

"Of course," Tiffany continued, "I didn't need him to tell me that, since Hilary came to see me."

"Did she?"

"Yes. I thought it very . . . civilized . . . of her. She came by my apartment to talk to me about the situation."

Sydney could only shake her head.

"She warned me that Richard would tire of me, one day, as he had of her."

Tiffany's amused expression showed that she didn't believe that. "Did she say *why* she was warning you? I mean, you are the other woman. . . ."

"Hilary said she was concerned for me. That Richard would hurt me. And she told me some nonsense about a man who cheats on his first wife would be more likely to cheat on his second. She said I would have done to me what I had helped do to her."

"It happens," Sydney said.

Tiffany's mouth curved into a smug smile. "Perhaps to other women. But Richard loves me. Our marriage will be different."

Sydney reserved comment, but she suspected that Hilary was right. In her estimation, Walker would never be content to stay with one woman.

The chase, the conquest, but never more.

He was, she thought, incapable of love.

Tiffany brushed her hair back over her shoulders. "I wonder if I should wait for him here?" she mused. "So that when he comes home. . . ."

Sydney recognized the proprietary air; Tiffany was settling in.

"It may be quite a wait," she said. She had turned to leave when a question occurred to her. "Tiffany, when did Hilary come to see you?"

"Monday."

"The day she disappeared?"

"Yes. That's why I think Richard is being foolish, worrying about all of this . . . I'm sure she's just taken off, to teach him a lesson. Absence makes the heart grow fonder. Or is it," she smiled archly "out of sight, out of mind?"

"Do you still think so?"

"Oh yes. She'll be back. No matter how civilized she is, she'd be a fool to give up without a fight. I certainly wouldn't."

That, Sydney believed. "What time did you see her on Monday?"

"About ten."

"Are you sure?" At ten, Hilary had reportedly been at the Mon Ami Salon.

"Absolutely. I'd gotten time off work and was waiting for a gentleman from the phone company to come and put in a new outlet, and when the bell rang, I thought it was he. I had a bit of a shock when I saw her standing there."

302

"My information is that Hilary was somewhere else at that time."

"Then your information is incorrect. She arrived a few minutes after ten and stayed for nearly thirty minutes."

"That's very interesting. Did you tell Dr. Walker about this?"

"It never came up. To be honest, I thought Richard would be angry if I told him what she'd said, and it would only make things worse. Besides, we had other things to talk about."

"I'm sure you did."

It was eleven p.m. by the time she got back to her office. The parking lot was deserted and the light from the street lamps didn't reach into all of the shadowed places.

Sydney unlocked the office door and went inside, feeling a measure of relief at finally being alone.

She had a lot of thinking to do.

She sat at the desk with all of the materials relating to the Walker case spread out before her. Reports, notes, tapes of interviews, and — propped against the in- and out-baskets — the photographs of Hilary.

Was Hilary Walker dead? The police thought so.

Looking at the face in the pictures, Sydney didn't want to believe it. There had to be an-

303

other answer, if only she could find it.

One by one, she reviewed every piece of evidence.

The case she had built, she realized, was a house of cards. Remove one, and they would all fall down.

From early in the case, she'd considered Richard Walker to be a liar. Their first conversation had planted the seeds of suspicion, and his every misstatement had nourished that suspicion, until now, it was in full bloom.

True, he had lied to her often—but in an odd way, by focusing her doubts solely on him, she had put blinders on. She had believed everyone else, had taken what they'd said at face value.

At least one other person had lied to her.

Philippe.

But why would he lie?

Sydney remembered his farm-boy good looks, the guileless smile.

Why not? she thought.

The salon might not give out the telephone numbers of its *artistes,* but perhaps Philippe had. Belatedly, she realized she'd never asked what his last name was, and she had to look at each page in both of Hilary's appointment books.

A listing for P. Matheson looked promising. She recognized the address as one of the more fashionable neighborhoods of La Jolla.

Sydney wanted to talk to him in person, but first she had to verify that he was home. If he answered, she would hang up without a word and show up on his doorstep, unannounced.

She dialed the number, and crossed her fingers for luck.

The voice that answered was familiar, but it wasn't Philippe's.

"Daphne," she said. He used the same answering service that she did. "It's Sydney."

"My heavens, Sydney, where have you been all day? And why are you calling on this line?"

"I'm trying to reach Philippe—"

"On a Friday night?"

So it *was* his number.

"I've never known the sweet boy to be home before daybreak," Daphne said, and laughed. "Where he gets the energy, I haven't a clue."

"Do you have any idea where I could find him? It's urgent."

"Well, I have a referral, but you know I'm not allowed to give it out—"

"Would you do me a big favor?"

"Sure, if it isn't illegal."

"Just dial the referral number and connect me ... I'll take it from there. They'll never know you were involved."

"You've got it."

Sydney had planned to improvise a story or whatever it took to get a name or address and track Philippe down, but when the phone was answered, the hint of an Irish accent in the woman's voice eliminated any need for that.

It was Mara Drake.

She hung up without a word.

THIRTY-EIGHT

Mara Drake did not appear surprised to see her, despite the lateness of the hour.

"Miss Bryant, how nice of you to drop by."

Sydney was not in the mood for playing games. "May I come in? I want to talk to you and Philippe."

"Oh, you know about that, do you? I shouldn't wonder, though. You're very persistent. And, I must admit, you're quite good at what you do. Finding that bastard McCullough couldn't have been easy."

"How did you—"

"Know about that? I know a great deal about many things. But do come in and join us. We were just having a taste of champagne. . . ."

Sydney followed Mara Drake to a trilevel living room where a fire blazed in the stone hearth. A glass wall allowed them a spectacular view of La Jolla Cove.

Philippe was standing by the fireplace, staring solemnly into the flames.

"We have company, Philippe," Mara Drake said.

His expression remained pensive, but he nodded. "Hello, Miss Bryant."

Mara Drake crossed to a small bar in the corner of the room and poured a glass of champagne, which she brought to Sydney. "I hope you'll join us."

Sydney accepted the glass but didn't drink. "Are you celebrating?"

Mara Drake's smile was enigmatic. "In a way, perhaps, but it will keep. You said you wanted to talk to us?"

"I have a few questions, if you don't mind. . . ."

"Not at all. Go right ahead. To be honest, there were a few things I may have failed to mention when we spoke the other day."

"I thought there might be."

"But you see, it was essential that you not find Hilary until, shall we say, the proper time."

"You know where she is?"

"Of course I know; she is my dearest friend." Mara sipped her champagne. "But first, ask your questions. I'm curious to hear what brought you back to us."

Sydney had to work at controlling her impatience; she wanted—even needed—to see Hilary Walker. But she sensed that Mara Drake would keep her secrets until it suited her to do otherwise.

"About Monday." Sydney glanced at Philippe.

"Hilary wasn't at the salon that day."

"No," Philippe said, "she wasn't."

"Why did you tell me she was?"

"It seemed the thing to do at the time." He downed his drink and put the glass on the mantel. "You were working for *him*, after all."

"By him, I assume you mean Richard Walker."

"Yes."

"So you lied."

"Yes, and I would do so again. Gladly."

"May I ask why?"

"As a favor to Hilary, and to protect her."

"How would lying about that protect her? And from what? I know where she actually was at ten that morning; she had gone to see—"

"Perhaps," Mara Drake interrupted, "I should be the one to explain. It was, after all, my idea. Philippe was only carrying out my orders."

Sydney looked from one to the other. "Your orders?"

"Yes, Miss Bryant. Are you sure you don't wish to sit down? It's rather a long story." She smiled again, and nodded. "I have no objections to answering your questions, now that it's almost over."

"What is almost over?"

"Why, the plan, of course."

"Miss Drake—"

"Call me Mara. My name actually is Margaret—Margaret Emily to be precise—but my mother thought that Mara had a little more class, more in keeping with my station. The only person who ever called me Margaret was Hilary.

Which, of course, brings us back to the reason you're here. . . ."

"Hilary."

The phone rang in another room, and Philippe glanced at Mara who nodded. He left to answer it.

"Now, what were you asking?"

"Why did Philippe bother lying about where Hilary was on Monday? What difference could it possibly make?"

"A great difference, really. We didn't want anyone to know about Hilary's visit to Richard's . . . lover . . . because then they would assume that Hilary had run away—"

"Which she had?"

"As you say. However, it was always out intention that Richard be suspected in her disappearance, which wouldn't be the case if it became known that she had knowledge of his affair. We couldn't have that, of course. Making it seem as though Hilary were some wounded bird taking flight."

Belatedly, Sydney remembered that neither Mara nor Philippe had given much credence to the rumors of discord in the Walker marriage. "So you hoped that by maintaining that *she*, at least, was happy, people would assume that something must have happened to her?"

"More or less."

"And the overall purpose of that was to implicate Walker?"

"Yes. That was the plan."

Philippe came into the room and went directly

to Mara's side. He whispered to her and she laughed with apparent delight.

"Very good," she said, "but there's no need for secrecy any longer, darling. I'm sure Miss Bryant would find it of interest as well; it appears that Richard has been unable to make bail this evening, and he'll have to spend the night in jail."

Sydney frowned. Given Walker's financial status and his professional standing in the community, bail should have been granted routinely.

"Ah, I know what you're thinking," Mara said. "Do you recall asking me if Richard had any enemies?"

"I do. You answered, 'None that I'm aware of.'"

Mara nodded. "You have an excellent memory. Actually, he has one, and in this instance, one is more than enough. *I'm* his enemy."

"And you've arranged to keep him from making bail?"

"Yes. It's quite simple. I have money, and money is influence."

"Which you also used to get the police interested in the first place." The pieces were beginning to click together in her mind.

"I managed to pique their interest, yes. It wasn't all that difficult ... the husband is usually regarded with suspicion in such cases."

"And the District Attorney?"

"I do believe he has political aspirations which he felt would be served by a successful prosecution in such a high-visibility case. I supported that decision, in order to assure a vigorous investigation."

"The press?"

Mara lowered her eyes in mock modesty. "Well, I did ask an acquaintance of mine to look into it. That was him on the phone just now. I believe you know him—"

"Victor Griffith?"

"Yes. He was initially supposed to follow you, to make sure you weren't on to us, but as it turned out . . . well, you know how it turned out. And since we're being honest, I may as well tell you that I had a friend run a background check on you, Miss Bryant. You'll be pleased to know that your reputation is an excellent one."

"But why? Why did you go to the trouble?"

"It was hardly any trouble at all. And as to why—as Philippe said—it was a favor to Hilary."

"A favor? All of the lies, the manipulation—"

"My intention was to give Richard a taste of his own bitter medicine. To show him how it feels to be publicly humiliated. He has always acted as though he was above judgement, but now he knows that isn't true. We have judged him, and found him guilty. . . ."

"You did all of that even though Richard Walker did nothing to harm Hilary?"

"But he did!" The outrage showed in Philippe's eyes. "He hurt her, and the other one—"

"Now, Philippe." Mara placed her hand gently on the young man's arm. "He's right, though. Hilary was grievously injured by Richard's indiscretions. Not physically, perhaps, but the worst

312

pain comes from the heart. And the affairs had been going on for several years, you see."

Sydney shook her head. "If she's known for that long, then why all of this now? And what did McCullough have to do with it?"

Mara Drake sighed. "Why now? Why *not* now. As for McCullough, yes, that was an unexpected complication. He threatened to ruin everything, with his ridiculous demands for money to keep his silence. But he got what had long been coming to him. . . ."

"The man is dead," Sydney said flatly.

"His death was divine justice to my way of thinking. Thomas McCullough very nearly killed Hilary when they were married; I have no sympathy to waste on him."

"All of that happened a very long time ago."

"Some things you can't forget, no matter how many years go by. There are wounds that never heal."

"Why did she go to see him?"

"To ask him to leave her alone, once and for all. She thought, rather naively, that he would show some compassion for her, since. . . ." Mara's voice trailed off until it was little more than a whisper. "It was a fool's errand, but I couldn't stop her."

Sydney felt a growing sense of dread. "Did she kill him?"

Mara didn't answer immediately, seemingly lost in thought, but after a moment she met Sydney's eyes. "I don't know . . . but he may have killed her, after all."

313

"I thought you said—"

"A few minutes ago, you asked me why we were doing all of these things, and why *now*. So I'll tell you. Hilary is dying, Miss Bryant. That C.T. in her appointment book? It stands for cancer therapy."

"She was receiving medical treatment?" How could Walker not have known?

But Mara Drake shook her head. "She has a brain tumor. Inoperable. There was no help for her ... no chemotherapy, no radiation treatments, nothing. The only therapy she had was that support group. A group of dying people comforting each other in face of the inevitable."

"I had no idea."

"No one did. After she was diagnosed, she went on with her life as usual. But now ..." Again her voice faded, and she glanced away.

Sydney waited.

When Mara looked back, her eyes had filled with tears. "Richard Walker will live, and Hilary will die. Her death will come as a relief to him, and I find that obscene. That, to me, is all the reason I need to do whatever it takes to see that he suffers along with her. She has lived a hard life, and now she's dying a hard death, but before she does, those who've hurt her will pay the price for what they've done."

"But you may pay as well," Sydney said. "There are laws against conspiracy."

"If I do, so be it. It seems a small enough favor to do for a dying friend."

"Will you tell me where she is?"

"I can't do that." Mara wiped at the tears. "And I won't."

Philippe, who had been listening silently, put his arm around Mara. "It's almost over," he said. "You'd best stay out of it."

Sydney thought that at last she knew where Hilary Walker was.

THIRTY-NINE

At six a.m. she slowed to make the turn onto the dirt road. A carved wood sign, nearly hidden by overgrown bushes, read, "Private Property, keep out."

This had to be the place. The land Hilary had inherited from her mother.

The Buick Sydney had rented at the San Francisco International Airport apparently needed new shocks; it bounced and shimmied over the ruts in the road until she thought the steering wheel would be wrenched out of her hands.

The early-morning sunlight slanted through the grove of redwoods and dappled the windshield, making it difficult to see. She lowered the visor. It didn't help.

A squirrel bounded across the road in front of her and she hit the brakes, the car's rear slewing sideways, narrowing missing a tree.

The engine stalled.

It would be easier, she decided, to walk the rest of the way.

Sydney got out of the car and stretched. She was tense from the trip north — she didn't like airplanes — and more than a little stiff from the drive from San Francisco to the Santa Cruz mountains. She rubbed the sore muscles in the small of her back as she walked along the road.

There had been no effort made to conceal the motor home. It sat in a small clearing, shaded by a half-circle of trees. The steady hum of a gas-powered generator grew louder as she approached.

Curtains closed off the driving compartment, but the rear windows were opened to the morning. The glass was tinted a smoky gray, but Sydney could make out a lone silhouette inside.

When she reached the door she took a deep breath and then knocked.

"Come in," a voice said.

Sydney's first thought was that Hilary Walker didn't look like either of her photographs.

Her auburn hair had been pulled back away from her face, which now seemed thinner, almost drawn, the skin stretched tight over her cheekbones. The area beneath her eyes looked bruised, and the pupil of her right eye appeared hazy, as though from a cataract.

Even so, Hilary Walker possessed an almost ethereal beauty.

She was dressed in a sweatshirt and faded jeans. The clothes hung heavily on her slight frame. She sat in the U-shaped lounge at the rear of the motor home, staring out the window. A steaming cup of tea was cooling on the table beside her.

Her hands were folded in her lap, but even from a distance, Sydney could see that they were shaking.

"Hilary?"

Hilary turned slowly in Sydney's direction, her mouth curving into a faint smile. "Do I know you?"

No, but I know you, Sydney thought.

"My name is Sydney Bryant," she said. "I'm a private investigator. Your husband hired me to find you."

"Well, you seem to have done that." She spoke quietly, without emotion.

"Mrs. Walker, I have a few questions to ask, if you don't mind."

"Why should I mind?" Her eyes drifted back to the window. "Even if you've come to take me back, there's nothing they can do."

"That isn't why I'm here." Sydney sat across from her. Up close, Hilary looked alarmingly pale. "Are you all right?"

"Yes, except for the fact that I'm dying." One hand went to her face. "And I can't see out of my right eye. Of course, the doctor warned me

318

that it might happen, but when it did. . . ."

"How long have you been—"

"Partially blind? Since Monday morning. But don't waste any sympathy on me. It's not as bad as I imagined it would be, waiting to die. It's rather peaceful, actually. But I'm sure you haven't come all this way to hold a death watch, have you?"

"No. I came to ask you for the truth."

Hilary's smile returned. "Am I the keeper of the truth? I wasn't aware of that."

"I think you are. You know what has happened in the past few days . . . and why."

"Why, indeed." She was silent for a moment. "If I tell you, I assume it will benefit Richard?"

"Yes, but it may help you, as well."

"I'm beyond help, I'm afraid."

"No one is beyond understanding."

Hilary did not seem to have heard her. There was a faraway look in her eyes. "Last summer," she said after a minute had passed. "It began last summer."

"In August. I started to feel ill. Headaches, blurred vision, an occasional dizzy spell. I thought at first I was just overtired, but when the symptoms worsened, I went to my doctor, and he sent me to a specialist, who ordered a series of tests."

"Dr. Walker didn't notice that you were ill?"

"If he did, he never mentioned it. And I saw

319

no need to say anything to him."

"Why not tell him?"

"Being married to a doctor opened my eyes to one of the many inequities of medical care. As a patient, I had, to some degree, relinquished my autonomy. That was bad enough, but I knew that if Richard was informed about my condition, I would have no further say in my own treatment. I couldn't allow that to happen."

"I see."

"The specialist diagnosed a malignant brain tumor, for which there was no hope of a cure, and told me I had six months to live."

Six months. August to February.

"The odd thing is, when he told me, I realized that it wasn't *death* he was sentencing me to ... but rather, for the first time in my life, I would really be free. And the six months wasn't how long I had left to live, but how much longer I had to wait for my freedom."

"You were that unhappy, that you considered death as a way out?"

"Yes," Hilary said simply.

"But why? I know that your marriage was failing—"

"It was over." Her smile was bittersweet. "In every way. We were strangers to each other. Polite but distant. Every time he made love to another woman, it was as if I didn't exist. He didn't even care if I knew. And when I found I was dying I realized that it wasn't just my marriage to Richard that had gone bad. My entire life has been a failure."

"I don't believe that."

"It's true. I used to think I was a survivor, that I could get through anything, but—" she shook her head, "—in the end, I knew I couldn't fool myself any longer. I hadn't survived . . . I'd only delayed the inevitable."

Sydney was silent.

"Did Mara tell you we went to Kenya last summer? It was hot and dry and magnificent. The days go by so slowly there. One day we happened upon a dead elephant. The hide, you know, is fairly thick. The body had wasted away, and all that remained was the hide and the skeleton. They say that after a while even the bones become brittle and can't support the weight, and they crumble into dust. All there is left then is the empty skin. And that's what will become of me. . . ."

"It doesn't have to be that way. There are people who care for you—"

All at once Hilary started to cough, and she reached unsteadily for the teacup, using both hands to lift it.

Sydney noticed a flesh-colored bandage on Hilary's right hand between the thumb and index finger. From where she'd cut herself on the broken glass? "Would you like to me take you to a doctor?"

"Thank you, but no." Her voice sounded raspy. "I've had quite enough of doctors."

Sydney could understand that.

"But you mentioned caring. Did you know, Miss Bryant, that I work with abused women?"

"Yes." She couldn't help but think of the photographs of Hilary she had in her shoulder bag. Abused seemed to be a mild way to describe what had happened to her.

"For a time I thought I might make a difference, that because I cared I could help them, but last summer I saw — very clearly — that I couldn't help them any more than I had helped myself. I watched one after another going through the same agony that I'd suffered. Enduring the physical abuse, taking the blame for it, as if it were something they'd said or done that caused what has happening to them. And always, always making excuses for their men."

Sydney thought of Gretchen Elliott's apparent inability to make the final break with her husband; of Annabelle Swann's flight from one man's arms into another's; and of Nina Munoz's declaration that her "friends" would protect her from the father of her children.

"I realized," Hilary continued, "that nothing I could say or do would ever really change anything. I can't help them . . . I can't even help myself."

"But you did . . . you divorced McCullough and you finally left Richard Walker."

"Yes, I left him." She looked down at her bandaged hand. "On Monday, when I lost the sight in one eye, I took it as a signal that the time had come to leave."

"Is that why you were crying that morning?"

"Yes and no. Crying because I've always feared being blind, and because I've never really *seen.*"

"You went to talk to your husband's mistress?"

Hilary nodded. "But it did no good. If anything, it will make her more determined to have him. Although she may prove to be his undoing. . . ."

Sydney thought it possible.

"I told Mara about it over lunch, and that's when we decided to do what we did. We went back to the house, had a glass of champagne, and then I broke the glass . . . and I . . . cut into my hand."

Sydney flinched.

"I let it bleed, to make it seem as though something had happened, and then we left."

"You took nothing with you?"

"I've never taken a dime from either man." She smiled grimly. "Perhaps if Richard had known I wouldn't ask for money, he would have ended the marriage years ago."

"Why didn't you end it?"

"I kept hoping he would tire of the other women. And then I was afraid. I don't know if you can understand that, but I was desperately afraid to be alone. Even a bad marriage . . . but it's over now."

"Yes, it is." Sydney hesitated. "Hilary, what happened between you and McCullough?"

"I ... it was an accident." What had started as a sigh ended as a gasp and her face contorted with pain. "I didn't want to kill him. . . ."

Was it the memory of what she'd done, or was she growing weaker? Sydney moved to Hilary's side and took her wrist to check her pulse. It beat irregularly.

"I'm going to get a doctor for you."

"No, please. I want to tell you. . . ."

Sydney got to her feet. "Where are the keys?" She'd drive the motor home to where she'd left the car and take Hilary into town.

"I didn't want it to happen, but I killed him. I asked him to leave me alone. I told him that I hadn't long to live, and he ... he laughed at me. He wanted to know what I'd left him in my will. That was all he cared about." A single tear fell from her sightless eye.

Sydney felt her throat tighten.

"And then he grabbed me, and tried to drag me into the bedroom ... for old times' sake, he said. But he was drunk, and he fell, and I saw the poker, and I hit him. Again and again, I hit him so hard that the wound on my hand tore open, and even then, I couldn't stop." Her face was ashen.

"Hush, now."

"Don't you see?" What little strength she'd had seemed to have drained out of her, and she closed her eyes. "I had no choice," she whispered.

Sydney found a ring of keys on a hook in the small kitchen. She poured the rest of Hilary's tea down the sink, and as she did so she noticed a chalky residue at the bottom of the cup.

"Damn it." There wasn't time to search for whatever Hilary had taken. She pulled back the curtains in front and tried two keys before she found the ignition key.

She nosed the motor home up to the Buick. Even as thin as Hilary was, she doubted that she would be able to carry her down the steps and put her in the car. Instead she backed the Buick off the side of the road and ran back to the motor home.

As she turned onto the paved road, she noticed a car coming in her direction slow and then pull off onto the shoulder.

She recognized the driver as she passed.

Karl Ingram sat next to her in the hospital waiting room. "How is she?"

"No one's told me yet." Sydney glanced at him. "I didn't know you were in on this, too."

"I wasn't, until yesterday. I got a call from a friend of Hilary's—"

"Mara Drake?"

"Yes. They needed someone to come up here with Hilary. She couldn't see well enough to drive." He looked down and away. "I would have done whatever they asked me. If only I'd been told sooner ... none of this would have hap-

325

pened. If only I had known. . . ."

If only, Sydney thought, Hilary had fallen in love with a decent man like Karl Ingram.

"I was supposed to take her to the motor home and then leave, but I . . . I got halfway down the mountain, and I had to turn back. I couldn't stand the thought of her being there, all alone."

"She's not alone now, Mr. Ingram," Sydney said.

FORTY

Sydney did not go to her office on Monday.
Tuesday morning when she arrived, Richard
Walker was waiting outside her door.

"Dr. Walker," she said.

"I wanted to talk to you."

"Then come in."

He looked, she thought, tanned and well
rested. Ethan had told her that after he was
released from jail, he'd gone to Palm Springs for
the rest of the weekend.

At last report, Hilary was in the Intensive
Care Unit at Dominican Hospital in Santa Cruz.
She was comatose, and the doctors weren't holding out much hope that she'd ever regain con-
sciousness.

Walker sat across from her and straightened
the crease in his pant leg. "I wanted to tell you
in person that I think you did an excellent job
in finding Hilary. I wasn't aware that she owned

327

any property—"

"No, I imagine not." What, she wondered, had he really known about his wife?

"At any rate, thank you."

Sydney inclined her head, but didn't speak.

"I've been wondering . . . Ethan said you talked to Hilary before she collapsed."

"Yes."

"Did she tell you why the elaborate hoax? If she was that unhappy—"

"You mean, why didn't she just shoot you and get it over with?"

Walker was clearly uncomfortable. "Well, yes, in a manner of speaking. Granted, she may have been not entirely of sound mind, considering the brain tumor, but it isn't like Hilary to be . . . vindictive."

"She felt you'd betrayed her. It was her way of fighting back."

"Oh, come now. A lot of men cheat on their wives, and they aren't set up as murderers. From what I understand, when the time came, Hilary intended to wander off into the woods to die. They might not have found her body for months, if ever. And I would have been punished for something I didn't do."

"Whatever her reasons for what she did, or tried to do, Hilary was as much of a victim as you were."

"I hardly think so."

His self-righteous attitude rankled her nerves. "What would have happened if Hilary hadn't disappeared? You were planning to divorce her. . . ."

"I'm sure we could have reached an adequate settlement, and then we both could have started over."

"You with Tiffany, and Hilary alone."

"That's life in the big city, Miss Bryant."

"She was dying."

He frowned. "It is unfortunate, but I'm not to blame for that."

"Do you know, Dr. Walker, that if you had noticed she was ill, all of this might not have happened? If you had cared to *see?* Don't misunderstand me — I don't approve of what she did — but how could you share a bed with Hilary, and yet fail to see that she was dying right in front of your eyes?"

"My actions are not at question here. I'm willing to forgive her, but I can't forget that my wife schemed with her friends to ruin my reputation, destroy my practice, and deprive me of my freedom."

Freedom.

The word brought the memory of Hilary as she'd last seen her, totally dependent upon the life-support machines that surrounded her bed.

"You're free now," she said.

Walker stared at her. "You don't like me, do you?"

"No, I don't."

"May I ask why?"

"Maybe because you're here and Karl Ingram is at Hilary's bedside."

"Who?"

"Never mind. It doesn't matter that I dislike you. You hired me to find Hilary and I did." She got up and went to the cabinet to get the case file. "Ethan told me that you've decided not to press charges against the others involved, and although I'm sure that it's your own reputation you want to protect, I'm glad that this will finally be over." She turned to face him.

Walker was silent, but he watched her warily as she walked toward him.

"Here's the file on Hilary, Dr. Walker." She handed the folder to him. "I don't usually do this, but I want you to have it. Maybe if you read it, you'll understand."

He took it gingerly, as though it might bite. "I appreciate this, Miss Bryant. I'll be honest . . . it made me a little nervous to think of such personal revelations being made public."

"I'm not doing it for you."

"Yes, I'm sure of that. Nonetheless, I *am* grateful."

"Don't be. Consider it a small favor . . . for Hilary."

"Still, I'd like to pay you for all of the extra trouble you've gone through." He brought out a checkbook and a gold pen. "Would ten thousand dollars be enough?"

Sydney blinked. "You can make the check out to Outreach. And then, Dr. Walker, you can get the hell out of my office."

When he'd gone she sat at the desk for a long

330

time.

The call came a few minutes after eleven. She listened to Karl Ingram's haunted voice, but she could think of nothing to say.

Freedom, she thought, and hung up the phone.